CH

Security guard 'Josh,' opened the gate, leaving just enough space for Professor Anita's 1970 Jaguar XJ which she had inherited when her father passed away recently, to squeeze through.

She wound down the driver's side window half way through. "Thank you, Josh."

Displaying her characteristic smile which could bring down any egoistic, dominant male to his knees. In appreciation of her kind gesture, Joseph the gate keeper saluted her with a dutiful heart. She pulled the old beast; yet with a majestic look and Herculean power generated by a 5-liter gasoline engine under its massive red bonnet, into the narrow space in between the two buildings.

She slammed the door heavily after getting out of the car and entered the building on the right side, through the very tall and broad door which was made of solid teak timber. On the wall, to the right side of the door, there was a spotlessly shiny copper board engraved in Century Gothic black letters; '**Department of Psychology.**'

As she walked in, she could smell the heady aroma of freshly brewed ground coffee, which stimulated her senses making her crave for a steaming cup. Though the door was wide, it led to a passage which was somewhat narrower. Her office was at the end of the passage.

On the door, hung a rather cheap plastic board, probably with laser cut letters, showing; Professor of Psychology – Anita

Wickramasooriya PhD, LLB and many more qualifications only a learned mind could identify.

"Good morning, madam."

"Good morning, 'Jine', did you make the coffee?"

"Yes, ma'am."

She punched in the digital lock of her office door which opened with a click. Even though the room was air conditioned, she preferred to keep the upward-sliding window three quarters opened, since she could drift into her own world of oblivion, blankly looking at the ancient tamarind tree outside the window and also letting in a bit of fresh air. Heavily painted metal rods kept any undesirables from gaining access to her office, though however, prying eyes would have had a heyday.

Her desk appeared untidy, although she thought she kept it exceptionally well organized, in a psychologist/psychiatrist's standard. She sat on the antique leather colonial era chair, yet again an item she insisted that she must have inherited from her deceased father.

She felt proud sitting on her father's office chair that he had used throughout his legal career, for many decades, until his demise at the 'not so old,' age of sixty-eight.

Every time she sat on it, she could virtually smell the old spice cologne and the aroma of the vanilla fragrance of Virginia tobacco this famous barrister used to smoke in his Vauen Auenland Shire Churchwarden pipe. Whenever she sat on it, she experienced a feeling of pride; a sense of closeness and affection toward her father, which she was never able to experience throughout her life.

Anita took the first sip of the steaming hot mug of coffee, dutifully made by the department peon, Jinadasa, commonly known as 'Jine'; almost burning her lips. It was a hot, Kopi Luwak

About the Author

Chrysantha Mendis is by profession a medical doctor who was born on 19 April 1956. Specialized in Anaesthesiology, he is currently (2023) holding the position of Clinical Director of the Heart Centre in a leading private sector Health Care facility in Sri Lanka. He qualified as a MBBS doctor in Sri Lanka and completed his Post Graduate education in the UK obtaining his FRCA (U.K) and FFARCSI (Irl). In the year 1994 he returned to his motherland to serve its people. He is very much an outdoor person who is interested in ecosystems, wildlife, bird watching, and angling. He is also an ardent animal lover.

Entreated Onus

Chrysantha Mendis

Entreated Onus

Olympia Publishers
London

www.olympiapublishers.com

OLYMPIA PAPERBACK EDITION

A CIP catalogue record for this title is
available from the British Library.

ISBN: 978-1-80439-721-3

First Published in 2024

Olympia Publishers
Tallis House
2 Tallis Street
London
EC4Y 0AB

Printed in Great Britain

Dedication

I dedicate this book to my wife and better half of me,
Suharshani, and my reason to live, my loving three daughters,
Anuka, Chiara, and Savani.

Acknowledgments

Thank you to my friend and mentor Capt. Elmo Jayawardena, who taught me A to Z of book writing and publishing. Last but not the least my proof reader and editor Desmond de Silva.

coffee (a coffee that consists of partly digested coffee cherries eaten and defecated by the Asian Palm Civet), gifted to her by her Aunt Rose who had visited Indonesia recently. She could feel the rich flavor flowing through her taste buds, when the phone rang rather loudly and rudely. From the rings, she knew it was an outside call, so she picked it up instantly.

"Good Morning, may I speak to Professor Anita Wickramasooriya?"

A somewhat husky voice with a distinct clarity and a confident authority, spoke on the other end. Being a top-class psychologist, she had this ability to distinguish the personality of a person by merely listening. One could say she was the world's authority on this subject, since 'Verbal Expression and Personality Traits,' was the thesis for her PhD, which she obtained from the most prestigious Deakin University of Australia.

"Yes, this is Professor Wickramasooriya speaking, may I know whom I am speaking to and regarding what?"

Her voice was strictly official and dominantly inquisitive; which had caused so many prospective future partners to run a mile, over the years.

"I am Senior Superintendent of Police, Ranga Fernando, from the Serious Crime Division." His tone was equally challenging and authoritative, Anita thought.

"How may I be of any assistance to the Police Department?"

"Madam, we need your help to profile a Pedophile who has brutally murdered a seven-year-old girl after raping her."

Anita just froze and in the process, spilled the coffee over her MacBook. Her head started to spin, and she was feeling squeamish.

"Madam, are you there?"

"Yes, yes, my apologies, I just spilled some coffee over my laptop." She mustered all the courage she had and tried to maintain her composure.

"Ma'am, hope you haven't burnt yourself."

"Oh no, it's just a few drops," she lied. The MacBook keyboard was drowning in very expensive coffee.

"Officer Fernando, what exactly do you need to know about this pedophile?"

"Professor it was reported only this morning and local police are conducting preliminary inquiries. The Coroner and JMO were informed. Both JMO and coroner have already visited the crime scene. DIG crimes has assigned me to oversee the investigations."

"Oh I see," her voice sounded terse.

She grabbed the tissue box on her desk, ripped out half the tissues in it and started mopping up the keyboard. However, her mind was elsewhere, digging up skeletons she had buried long years ago.

SSP Ranga realized that he should not waste this professor's valuable time.

"Professor, as soon as I get the preliminary report I will send it over to you. Thank you very much, do you think you can assist us on this? If you could do that, the Police department will be grateful to you."

In his heart he knew his conversation with Prof. Anita was not just a simple official matter. The departmental secretary walked into Prof. Anita's room.

"Madam, you have a lecture at ten a.m. at the Medical Faculty and again your monthly session for the drug addicts at the General Hospital psych unit, at two p.m."

"Thank you Trish, did you do that letter to Family

Counselling Bureau?" "I'll do it now."

Anita's conversation with Theresa, the secretary, was a mere automatic response, since her learned mind was traveling at God's speed without a clear direction. Then she realized she was sweating like a pig, drenching her exclusive 'Kate Middleton,' underwear. The goosebumps which sprang up whilst listening to SSP Ranga, started gradually disappearing.

She was digging into her past. The way she did it would have put the famous archaeologist William. F. Albright to shame.

Whilst her mind ventured instinctively into her past which was locked away safely in a place like Fort-Knox all these years, her sharp and penetrating, beautiful black eyes were focusing on the desk calendar in front of her.

On the top of the calendar, she noticed July 2022.

CHAPTER 2

"Ensa, when you are removing the cobwebs from the ceiling, tear off the page of the kitchen calendar,"

Ensahamy, the faithful and lifelong 'live-in' domestic help of the 'Wickramasooriya Walauwa,' (mansion), removed the top page of the calendar, which was hung on the kitchen wall.

The top of the page of the calendar showed 1988 February.

Wickramasooriya Walauwa was situated on a picturesque mountain top, surrounded by a vast tea plantation owned by the famous Barrister, George Wickramasooriya. Barrister Wickramasooriya, who claimed that his bloodline traced back to Ceylon royalty, had inherited vast extents of land donated by the king, for the bravery shown by his ancestors.

The 'lady of the house,' Helen, was short; four feet eleven inches to be exact, and very petite.

She never admitted that she was below five feet in height. She always insisted that she was five feet tall and nobody dared to challenge her. Hailing from an aristocratic family in Sri Lanka, Helen was the only heir to her parents,' massive wealth, consisting mainly of real estate. She had her secondary education as a boarder at The King's School, Canterbury, in the UK. At the time, her mother Philomena, was doing her English degree at Oxford.

At the same time, Anita's father George Wickramasooriya, was doing his Barrister's examination after obtaining an LLB from Cambridge.

Having seen young and handsome George who was twenty-five years of age then, at a social function, Philomena thought she found the ideal match for her daughter Helen, who was celebrating her seventeen birthday. With this future plan in mind, Philomena always kept in close contact with George.

Philomena obtained a PhD in English and returned to Sri Lanka with her nineteen-year-old daughter Helen, who had been boarded at Canterbury. More or less at the same time, George too returned to Sri Lanka, after finishing his Barrister's.

The marriage of Helen and George ensued in a grandiose style, in Sri Lanka. Helen was so impressed with George, even though it was effectively an arranged marriage; which was the norm those days, especially in high society and Royalty alike. The modus operandi was to frequent exclusive clubs, societies and high-class sports events, to meet prospective partners.

Helen fell in love with George from the very first day she saw him in England. George was somewhat dark, as an average SriLankan man would be. However, he had the advantage of height, a large frame, sharp features and above all, 'smooth talk,' with the ladies. He was a maestro, surpassing any world-renowned Romeo in love. His speech was irresistible to any female of eight to eighty years of age.

The added qualifications of wealth, education and a claimed Royal bloodline, raised him up as a formidable contender to be the 'most eligible bachelor,' of that era in Sri Lanka. In marriage however, George was a passionate lover, dutiful husband, honorable man and a responsible Father.

Anita was born even before nine months into their marriage. So, it was necessary to say she was a premature baby. However, the gynecologist's and pediatrician's notes indicated a 'full term,' baby. At the christening of the baby, a few inquisitive high society ladies were seen mumbling secretly and laughing out loud, though the tone was friendly, and with a show of acceptance.

Helen started blushing when George's only uncle, Henry, came and tapped on George's back and said, "Good old chap, you seem to take after your old man, you are not anywhere near your brother, Congratulations my boy!"

With this comment, Helen was somewhat perturbed but decided to keep quiet. However, she saw her husband's expression changing from extreme bliss to a somewhat worried face. With plenty of premium single malt, Macallan forty-year-Old and Domaine Leroy Vintage 1947 red wine, flowing by the gallons that day, everyone forgot about everything else and 'drowned,' themselves in this fine quality yet unbelievably expensive, liquor.

That was a day to remember, though baby Anita, on the other hand, was craving for her mother's nipple for her share of milk.

Helen was just the young and shy mother of newly born Anita, though associating with boisterous, high echelons of the then society, trying to digest what they said in their alcoholic stupor.

"George doesn't seem to be anywhere near his brother."

What George's only uncle told him whilst tapping him on his shoulders, echoed in Helen's mind repeatedly, torturing her. Helen thought his uncle was drunk and had mixed up his words while referring to some other person.

Anita started crying continuously and the nanny was unable to pacify the six-week-old baby. So, Helen excused herself from the loud and drunken crowd and took the baby to seek refuge in the master bedroom where the baby's cot was kept.

Baby Anita, after drinking her fill of milk from her mother's breast, fell asleep while still hanging on her mother's nipple. Helen gently placed the baby in the cot and covered her with the mosquito net. She could hear the muffled sounds of voices, laughter, piano music and singing. She did not want to join the party. She too fell asleep on the bed in her expensive, long black Gucci dress.

Not even thirty minutes into her sleep, Helen suddenly woke up and realized she hadn't even changed. She took a warm water shower and put on her polka dot cotton nightdress. Baby Anita was fast asleep, probably dreaming of her mother's milk. Helen was tired.

She got on to the bed and covered herself with a Peter Do Teddy, wool-silk blanket. She felt the warmth spreading through her body, easing off a heaviness of her head and a very mild headache. About fifteen minutes later, she realized sleep had abandoned her.

Uncle Henry's remark,

"You are not anywhere near your brother," kept tormenting her, because as far as Helen knew, George only had a sister who was a good ten years younger to him living in Colombo and had no other siblings. She was turning and tossing for hours when the 'Howard Miller,' Grandfather clock near the teak staircase landing, chimed thrice, indicating that the time was three a.m. From the absolute silence around, she assumed the party snobs must have gone home.

Then she heard the gentle opening of the bedroom door and saw George walking in erratically, bumping into the clothes rack and grabbing his pajamas. She pretended that she was asleep. With the greatest difficulty, George managed to change into his pajamas and just collapsed onto the bed. He quickly got under the blanket and kissed Helen's forehead gently.

"Good night, darling."

A strong alcohol smell and tobacco fragrance, filled the room instantly. She always loved the vanilla essence, Virginia tobacco aroma. However, she had the greatest aversion toward the alcohol smell.

The baby got up twice during the night for her share of mother's milk. The whole of the following day was melancholy for the Wickramasooriya family. Since they were too tired, they were basically sleeping the whole time.

However, Helen's mind was not at ease until she got the clarification for that statement. George was not himself, probably thinking about that too.

The day after, at the breakfast table, Helen confronted her husband. "George what was the meaning of "you are not anywhere near your brother? You have no brother."

George literally froze!

However, being a Barrister, he did not have much difficulty in countering his wife's interrogation, though Helen noticed the guilty feeling in her husband's body language.

"I had a younger brother who was very mischievous but he met with a tragic death, our family couldn't take it, so we decided to bury that memory with him. Especially my mother, was heart-broken. So, my father ordered us never to mention anything about him or his death."

"Furthermore, even we were not told where he was buried or exactly how he died." Helen did not buy the last sentence.

When she was about to ask something else, George got up and said in a firm voice.

"I expect in this household, never to speak about that ever, do I make myself clear?" and walked off.

The Judge had given his judgement and no one could

challenge that. For the next year or so, neither of them talked with each other, nor even looked at each other. Helen's mind was engulfed in a thick black cloud which never cleared from that day onwards. George was not the same lovable and pleasant man from that moment.

It was like building the Great Wall of China instantly, separating Helen and George. Life was never the same afterwards at 'Wickramasooriya mansion.'

Though George tackled the initial inquiry reasonably well without leaving blatant loose ends, he knew this wouldn't stop there, and it would surface again and again in different ways like a carbuncle, in years to come. Like his loving wife, he too had quite a few sleepless nights over this.

George thought he was better than Abrie Krueger of South Africa, considered the most notorious liar, and sometimes even checked his nose to see whether it was growing longer like Pinocchio's.

Being a man of law and justice, he knew that one day, the truth would come out no matter what. Even though the dark side of the 'Wickramasooriya clan,' had been swept under the carpet by power, money and connections, his legal mind knew it was a 'fairy tale like,' illusion.

This kept on haunting his strong personality, reducing him to a mediocre soul. Being a time-tested fighter, George argued within his own mind, like he did in a Supreme Court, to decide on the best defense he could muster.

However, every now and then, his own defensive arguments melted away like butter in a frying pan with the full flame on!

This Wickramasooriya vs Wickramasooriya debate went on for almost one year and the 'living Wickramasooriya,' lost his case.

The confession of the guilty party is the desired outcome in a conflict of sorts. Meanwhile, baby Anita was growing up to be a bit of a handful and was needing a lot of attention and affection. He thought they had been living an estranged life for long enough and the baby needed them both to care for her as a loving couple.

George made up his mind and decided to divulge the truth. However, he knew he was going to divulge the information necessary, only as a 'damage control,' on a 'need-to-know,' basis. This decision was to chase away the 'Wickramasooriya Clan Ghost,', so he could establish some sanity within himself and to pacify his loving wife who was drifting away from him.

It was a bright and sunny Saturday. He had asked the butler to prepare the breakfast table on the perfectly manicured lawn, overlooking the distant mountains.

"Darling would you join me for breakfast today? I need to speak to you."

He mustered his hidden charm and quite confidently imparted these words. Even before the words came out, Helen knew George was begging for this moment.

Helen was wearing her 'floral,' dressing gown which was the standard attire SriLankan older generation 'society housewives' wore at home. George was wearing blue corduroy pants and a cream-colored polo neck, long sleeved T shirt.

"Helen darling, please accept my apologies, that day, when you asked about Edward, I was very rude to you. If you like to know, I can explain everything."

"I have all the time in the world. Go on."

She poured herself a cup of tea and had a sip. Then she took a slice of toast and started applying butter on it.

"When my mother got married, she was only nineteen years

of age. I was the eldest in the family and Edward was born three years later. Rose was born seven years after Edward.

We grew up in our estate. Edward was always different and was fond of killing animals even when he was five years of age. He was a loner and liked to play by himself and spent most of the time in the estate. My father never really liked him and he was given a kind of step-brotherly treatment by him. My mother was very protective of Edward and defended him all the time.

Even when there was a rumor that he was not a son of my father, but was the child of a famous Arabian horse trainer at the turf club; I of course, loved him because he was always there for me and we did so many things together.

Once, I can remember, he beat up a classmate of mine who was a big bully. Even though Edward was three years younger to me, he challenged this bully and beat him up in the playground in front of the whole school, during the interval. He was also very good with his catapult and never missed a target.

When I was fourteen and he was eleven years of age, something terrible happened. He beat up another big boy who called him an Arab. During this skirmish, he had pushed him over a rock and he had fallen about 20 feet, broken his neck and died instantly. He disappeared that day and we never saw him again."

Helen was still applying butter on the first slice and she just looked at George with wet eyes.

It wasn't the butter but it was her heart which was melting this time, listening to her loving husband. She was feeling guilty, she had suspected her husband without knowing the real facts.

Wiping the tears from the corner of the napkin, "So, what happened to him?" she asked.

"Up to date, we don't know. My father, over the years, went

and inspected many unidentified bodies without any success."

"My mother never recovered from that tragic incident and confined herself inside the house since then. Our sister Rose was only four years old at the time and we never told her anything about Edward. We sent her to Colombo to be looked after by a faithful 'Nanny,' and to attend school from there."

Helen placed her hand over George's hand and squeezed it gently.

"Sorry darling, you have gone through a lot and I am really sorry for what happened to your family, forgive me for making an issue out of some loose words from a bad mouth."

She noticed a single teardrop appearing in George's eye. At that very moment, their eternal love was revived like letters carved on a granite rock, never to fade away. Maybe, it was the best breakfast they ever had together.

CHAPTER 3

Michael Warnayaka woke up from a traumatic dream, to see his traditional dark blue and brown striped pajama drenched in his own sweat. He opened the huge patio doors and walked into the humongous balcony overlooking the spectacular valley below. He could see miles and miles of 'mountainy,' landscape. Michael automatically looked at his Rolex Oyster Perpetual he had bought in Oxford Street, in London, more than thirty years ago.

As a habit, he never removed the watch. Underneath, the skin area covered by the strap was pale and white, somewhat resembling a dirty pearl against his natural brown skin. He always thought it was his best identification mark, even surpassing DNA testing, in the event he died in the middle of nowhere.

The time was 6.37a.m. in the morning. He was barefoot, so he felt the coldness of the Calacatta Bettogli marble laid across the balcony, which he had personally imported from Italy, after visiting the factory.

The frigid marble imparted a soothing feeling to his feet, which traveled up to his psychopathic mind.

He forgot to wear the luxury dressing gown he had bought from Harrods of London. Suddenly, he felt the cold grappling with his whole body, like an octopus trying to squeeze him. Though he wanted to go in and put on his dressing gown, his deranged mind had other devious ideas.

He walked up to the floor mounted Celestron Edge HD1400 XLT professional telescope, which he had ordered personally from Torrance, California, USA. It was firmly floor mounted on the left side of the balcony, overlooking the tea estate workers' quarters, far away.

His eagle eyes caressed the eye-piece of the telescope, bombarding his psychopathic mind with images of little children playing in front of their houses down below. Seeing the little children playing, his whole body started to relax and a sense of euphoria engulfed his soul.

The Celestron fourteen-hundred telescope was so powerful, one could even visualize the finer details of the facial expressions of subjects seen as far as two miles away.

Michael was ecstatic and enjoying the view. He forgot that he was cold. "Sir, can I bring your bed tea?"

Nicolaus the 'Appu,' his butler's voice reverberated in his ears, rudely interrupting his near visual orgasm.

"Appu, bring my breakfast without the bed tea today, on to the balcony."

With this interruption, he suddenly felt the cold which was like someone pouring liquid nitrogen all over the body. That reminded him to go back to his room and put on his 'much treasured,' dressing gown. On the other side of the spacious balcony, there was a white painted, cast-iron square table with traditional 'Rose flower,' designed edges and four equally matching chairs.

Michael went inside the room, enjoying the warmth of the room air, until his butler laid down the breakfast on the balcony table outdoors. First, Nicolaus wiped the table top and the four chairs, which were coated with a thin layer of mist and placed a soft cushion on one of the chairs facing the view below. Then he hurried back to the side entrance stairs of the balcony. Just below the master's bedroom was the eighteen-place dining hall.

Through the dining hall, he walked toward the kitchen. His wife Justinahamy, had already prepared their master's breakfast.

She placed the oversized antique ebony tray which was very heavy, on the kitchen table which was comparatively modern. She had been performing this morning ritual all these years without fail, even if she was ill. Two fried eggs sunny side up, fried tomato, two rashers of lean bacon, two slices of toast, two dollops of Seville Orange marmalade, freshly made orange juice, plus water melon, papaya or any other available fresh fruit and Coffee brewed in a vintage Manning Bowman, silver coffee pot, was his breakfast of choice. Michael preferred Greek coffee cups over vintage 'British Royal design,' coffee cups. A somewhat oversized, tailor-made napkin, made of 'Pima,' cotton imported from Peru, was folded into a triangle, kept always to the right side of the tray.

A strong pair of hands could manage to carry the fully laid tray.

However, the difficult part was to carry it through the dining area and then up the precariously narrow spiral staircase, to the outside balcony.

Enormous skill and experience was needed to negotiate the circular stairway without toppling the heavy tray. Nicolaus the butler, had done it thousands of times over the years, so he was quite adept at it.

When he approached his master who was seated on the chair overlooking the valley down below, he noticed his happy and lively face, which he had seen only rarely.

"Appu, I'll take 'Red Rum,' for a ride, tell Banda to saddle her up."

A sixth sense told him his master would take the mare for a

ride today, so he excused himself from his master and disappeared from the balcony. At the bottom of the spiral stairway, he entered the perfectly manicured lawn with Japanese lawn grass and walked toward the stables which was one level below the lawn. He walked down the natural granite block steps and reached the sandy area in front of the stables.

Though the original 'Red Rum,' was sired by an Arabian thoroughbred, one cannot say this Red Rum was anywhere near a thoroughbred extract. The name was copied by Michael's father from the famous one, not-withstanding the fact that it was a male. This Red Rum had never ever gone anywhere near a racing track. However, in the early days, she was sent for a training stint at the Royal Turf Club, Nuwara Eliya. After assessment by expert trainers, it was decided that Red Rum was not racing material.

So, she was taken back to the 5000-acre tea plantation which belonged to the 'Nayaka's clan,' of the aristocrats from Kandy. This was Michael's estate where Red Rum was raised.

Steep slopes and orderly grown tea, planted by the English planter Randolph Strafford in the eighteenth century, made this young horse to be the finest transportation mode in this rugged mountain terrain. Her forte was negotiating rocks, climbing steep slopes and walking through the narrow winding tracts without even stumbling. She was the Queen of the tea estate.

Red Rum was Michael's love, and she acknowledged that every time he came near her, with a lovable 'Neigh.' Michael had been riding Red Rum throughout the estate for many years. Together, they were a formidable riding duo which explored every inch of this vast tea estate.

'Banda,' the stable hand, was brushing the horse down when Nicolaus reached the open stable door.

"Master wants to ride the horse; can you saddle the horse?"

When Banda raised his head, he saw 'Appu,' walking away as if he was nonexistent.

Banda never liked Appu. In his view, Appu had a 'stiff upper lip,' which was a sign of the bogus apishness acquired by the butler, all because he was the only one in the household who had the opportunity to converse directly with the master. None of the staff on the estate liked Appu.

However, everybody loved their master, since he was a kind man who was generous toward his staff.

Michael Warnayaka was a five foot eleven inches tall, broad-shouldered person. He had a beautiful large 'Arabian extract,' nose. It was rumored that he was the love child of an Arabian who was breeding thoroughbreds at the Turf Club. Even though his sharp features and penetrating black eyes were irresistible to women, he was never interested in the feminine gender.

He was known as a philanthropist who donated many things to society and was a very respectable landowner in that area. People realized that he did not desire popularity and prominence.

However, he was rumored to have been in a cult similar to 'Freemasons.' Having first appeared on the estate as a young adult on his return from England, he was an extremely private person, associating with very few people and those also, not from the area he lived. He never traveled much and was hardly seen in the surrounding towns and villages.

He was somewhat of a 'mystery man,', yet everyone knew he would come to their aid if and when they needed him. A man of few words, he never gave away any clues by which to judge his character. From the time he arrived, he 'confined,' himself in this vast stretch of land and appeared to be quite happy and content to do so.

He was referred to as 'Michael Hamu,' by the surrounding villagers. He had an impeccable character and was a highly respected individual in that area.

He owned a 1927 Rolls Royce Phantom; which people claimed was a priceless vintage car, since it was in good running condition. In addition to that, he used his red 1959 MG MGA sixteen-hundred Cabriolet for his rare exertions to surrounding towns.

He was the savior of the poor people living in that locality, if and when disaster fell upon them. He was quite generous and very caring.

Throughout his life, 'Michael Hamu,' had shown his class and refinement by his life style, and how he conducted himself whenever he interacted with society. Anyone who met him loved the person behind that handsome persona, instantly. He was doted on by everyone who knew him.

The only exception was the opinion of the ladies who had rare acquaintances with him. Though some slandered him as 'Gay,' there was not a single shred of evidence to substantiate such a claim. If such a claim was made, even if backed by any 'evidence,' Michael would have proven that he was not a homosexual by far, through his life style.

A few ladies of the higher society were eternally trying to rope him in for a romance. However, no one had a second chance to meet him privately or even to speak to him personally, except on a social matter. Since he was pleasant and lovable, nobody dared to label him as 'weird,' so they settled for the word 'Mysterious.'

Michael was wearing his cream-colored jodhpurs and a

hundred percent Lambswool, Scottish Shetland sweater which had the Shetland signature pattern. As soon as Red Rum saw the master in riding attire, carrying the braided leather hunting crop and wearing his worn-out black jockey skullcap; she knew that today the master would be riding her for a while. Michael came near the mare and rubbed her jaw below the right eye gently, "Would you care to take me to the jungle patch, my girl?"

Red Rum also responded to that with her typical neigh of approval and excitement. They were a perfect riding duo, sharing many a secret over the years.

About 500 acres of his vast estate of 5000 acres, was virgin jungle which continued as a wilderness, to form a nature reserve which extended for about 15 kilometers. There were no perimeter fences or land marks, except survey department archives indicating a minor mountain top and a few small streams flowing through the estate.

Though the mare's name was Red Rum, Michael liked to call her "Doodle". Michael mounted "Doodle" with much confidence, knowing his weight of 75 kilograms was not too heavy for this fine specimen of an equine!

"Ok love, to the forest patch."

Her low-pitched rumbling and snorting sounds indicated Red Rum understood where her master desired to go. It started with a slow walk followed by short spells of trotting, where the path was steady and wide. There was no room for cantering or galloping, due to the steep terrain. This duo, in harmony, negotiated the low-cut tea bushes with much finesse and reached the jungle patch within fifteen minutes.

It was an entirely different kettle of fish when it came to going through this virgin forest where the undergrowth was unpredictable and merciless. It was strewn with rocks, large boulders, rotting tree trunks covered with moss and lethal muddy pools, covered with thick vegetation. "Doodle" had the ability to smell danger and negotiate all the obstacles safely.

Once they entered the jungle patch and when they were out of sight from the estate side, Michael dismounted from the mare.

"My love, it's time to put your lovely boots on," and he took out a strange, tailor-made hoof cover which he himself had made from a sambar hide and had never been seen by anyone at the estate.

It was basically a small sac which covered the entire hoof and extended up to about 5 inches up the leg. A shoelace was attached to the top end and once worn over the hoof, the lace could be tightened with a simple knot, securing it tightly, so that it would not fall off even if the horse was galloping. In his leather shoulder bag, Michael had four of those. Red Rum was used to the ritual, and she appreciated the covers, since small pebbles and thorns would not get stuck in her hooves.

Even without prompting, through sheer habit, she raised her legs one by one, letting her master put on her boots.

Once done, Michael kissed Red Rum's forehead, "Doodle you are my confidante; I wish I could marry you." He mounted the mare in an instant, "OK girl, let's go to our playground."

Doodle was navigating her master through the jungle, making sure tree branches would not touch him. Actually, there was no footpath as such, since Michael ensured that he took several different routes to reach his 'playground.' They crossed three narrow streams and at every stream, Michael made it a point to wade in it for at least 100 meters, before getting out from the opposite bank, so no one would could trace him easily.

About thirty minutes later, through the virgin forest, they reached Michael's secret playground. This jungle patch was the continuation of a nature reserve, where sambar, wild hogs, deer and leopards habituated. The advantage of riding a horse in this territory was that the horse could smell the danger of the presence of a leopard. It was one of the perimeter boundaries by a fairly large stream, about 20 to 30 feet wide, with many boulders strewn around. Except on a heavily rainy day, one could cross the stream by jumping from boulder to boulder. However, when the stream was angry and muddy colored, no one could cross it, unless their intention was to commit suicide.

About 200 meters away from the stream, in the jungle patch, there was a big boulder which was about 30 feet in height and with a kind of recess similar to a cave, at the bottom of it. This was Red Rum's resting place when her master played in his imaginary playground. Due to the thick vegetation, the place where Red Rum rested was never visible from the other side of the stream. On that side, about 300 meters away from the stream at a higher elevation was the estate laborer's quarters.

From Michael's bungalow, one could see the terraced houses which the laborers occupied, since those were at a higher elevation. However, the stream was not visible from the bungalow. This shallow stream with clear water, was the spot where the estate workers bathed and washed clothes and the children frolicked.

Once they reached the hideout, Michael dismounted and walked on the rock face of the recess, bent down and went right in. He had to crawl the last few feet, so he could reach the hole at the end of the recess, which he has had covered with a flat rock. He moved the rock to a side, put his hand into the hole and grabbed the plastic bag inside it. He took the bag and came out of the low roofed area.

Michael sat on the rock face and emptied the contents. The

plastic bag contained shoe covers, an olive-green sarong and a shirt, a wig and a pair of spectacles. He put on his own shoe covers which were also of Sambar hide made by himself.

The sole of this hide was glued with neatly fashioned wild boar hooves, just thick enough to make hoof marks. So, when he walked about, it appeared as if wild boars were loitering around. Ingenious in disguise, he would remove his riding cap and put on the jungle green sarong and a plain shirt of the same color.

A pair of cheap spectacles with plain glass lenses he pulled out of the bag, was similar to spectacles donated by charitable projects. Then he wore a wig with jet black hair. With all these disguises, no one could identify him easily, except from his height. He then walked with a hunch, so his height was not prominent.

Then he took out a bird whistle which imitated the call of a peacock.

CHAPTER 4

Police constable Punyasiri tapped timidly on the door, "Sir, may I come in?"

A gruff, low toned voice answered "Yes."

PC 'Punya,' hesitantly open the door which was not locked. As soon as he walked in, he stood at attention and saluted SSP Ranga Fernando, whom he had thought would be much older. He wanted to say,

"Sir, you are so young," but decided otherwise. Ranga was the youngest SSP he had seen in his thirty-five years of service. SSP Ranga had taken up his post recently.

"Sir, you have a confidential file from the Central Province DIG's office."

"Ah yes," his voice was both receptive and authoritative. PC Punya handed over the file and while still facing the SSP, took a step back, saluted again and left.

"Please close the door behind you." Neither a "thank you," offered, nor expected.

Ranga was waiting for this file so he could probably go and meet Prof. Anita in person. His whole body awakened. His brain started pouring out gallons of love hormones, dopamine and serotonin, which led to an increase in oxytocin in his blood. A sense of confidence enveloped his mind and his body was aroused and ready for action.

He opened the file and started reading it attentively. He wanted to impress the professor, so he knew he had to be thorough with the case. He was so engrossed with it that when someone tapped on the door, even without lifting his head, he said "I am busy"

Then the person who tapped on the door, pushed it open slightly,

"Sir I am IP Silva; we have arrested three people from that drug case," without even looking at him or inviting him inside the room,

"Silva, you can handle that, I have a serious case,"

"OK. Thank you sir, I'll attend to it"

Ranga heard the door closing. He picked up the phone and rang the receptionist WPC Geetha. "Geetha don't send anyone to see me, I am going out soon."

He kept on reading. He was highly engrossed with the gruesome murder of a seven-year-old girl in Central province. He thanked God that this case was passed over to him, as his prayers were answered; because this was a golden opportunity to meet the professor in person, face to face, though he had a fairly insignificant acquaintance with her during the Convocation Ceremony of the University of Colombo the previous year, when he received the PhD. He was the first ever Police Officer to be conferred with a PhD in a rather unusual topic of 'Criminal Mind Pathways.' It was a research-based PhD which analyzed gruesome criminal activities that had happened in Sri Lanka over the last ten years. Based on actual criminal activities, a 'Criminal Mind Profile Algorithm,' was researched by him.

Whilst reading, SSP Ranga concentrated on the finer details of the incident, since he anticipated a barrage of questions from the renowned professor. He was even seeking the answers to possible hypothetical questions that may be raised by Professor Anita.

Personally, this was a crusade in impressing the Professor, rather than actually seeking a profile of the rapist cum murderer of this child of seven years. In his whole life, he had never read any report with this magnitude of concentration.

He pushed down on the age-old desk top office bell, a reminder of the colonial past of Ceylon; which was probably used by the very first Chief Superintendent of Police, William Robert Campbell in year 1866. It was a copper alloy bell with a character of its own and a distinctly loud sound of an 'F' note. When someone rang it, it was said that it could be heard in every nook and corner of the building.

The very next moment, WPC Geetha entered the SSP's office even without knocking on the door. She just couldn't get her eyes off this young, tall and hunky Police Officer. She stood to attention, keeping a 'back straight and bosom up' posture and dutifully saluted her superior officer.

"Yes Sir, you called?"

"Geetha, can you please ring the Faculty of Medicine, Department of Psychology and get an urgent appointment with Professor Anita for me to see her today, regarding the murder case? She knows what it is about."

"Yes Sir, consider it done."

She turned round fast as if she were on a cat walk and walked slowly in a rhythmic pattern with swaying hips. Every WPC knew SSP Ranga had a desire to watch the ladies walk, especially when they were walking away from him.

These are the secret things women in general notice about men. Men on the other hand, are totally ignorant about the fact that women sense these hidden passions even when they are looking the other way.

He was nervously playing with the cheap ball point pen

which was given to all Police Officers, tossing it between his fingers without even realizing it. Then a single drop of sweat on his broad forehead dropped on to the file. The cheap off-white paper of the report swallowed the sweat drop instantly, though Ranga tried vainly to mop it off with his thumb. Even though only a few minutes had passed, he felt as if it was hours. Then he heard a gentle tap on the door.

"Come in please."

"Excuse me Sir," it was the much hopeful Geetha with her best inviting smile.

"Sir, Professor asked you to come at two p.m. sharp, since she has a lecture at three p.m. She asked me to inform you to bring a photocopy of the report for her reference."

Even though it was not normally permitted,

"Geetha, can you photocopy this for me but don't enter in the log book."

With her flirty look, she whispered "All right Sir, I'll do exactly the way you request," and disappeared.

With a sense of relief, Ranga stood up and walked toward the massive window which was never opened. The colonial era window had small lattice type square glass pieces, supported by a teak frame. Probably, the window had never been cleaned from outside. However, nature was so kind that every time it rained, the window was cleaned naturally by the rain drops. Through a layer of dust, Ranga looked at the road below. Though he was looking at the busy road below, nothing was registering in his mind. He was recapitulating how to start the conversation with Prof. Anita.

The Frank Hope-Jones vintage wall clock with a handcrafted oak frame, which was hung over Prof. Anita's office entrance door, chimed at two p.m. sharp. Then she heard the tap on the door. She was going through her MacBook notes but she instinctively knew it was the Police Officer.

"Come in please," in her somewhat British accent she had acquired during her Cambridge days.

Then she saw the tall figure entering the room with much confidence. She had a vague recollection of having seen him before but was visualizing a person of an average height, dark, with a stereotype typically 'police face,' without a hint of a smile.

She was completely wrong!

There he was, a tall, broad-shouldered, somewhat curly haired, clean shaven police officer with a cheerful smile. It took a few seconds for her nervous system to re-program her memory to adjust to the new image of this police officer – smile scenario!

She had never seen an Immigration Officer or a Police Officer on duty, smiling, in her whole thirty years of life.

SSP Ranga took his peaked cap off and chucked it between his left upper arm and chest. Then he saluted her.

"I believe you are SSP Ranga Fernando."

She made a valiant attempt to muster a 'British Royal,' accent. "Yes Ma'am."

Being a psychologist, she realized that the SSP was very nervous, in spite of his smile. However, she was at a loss for reasons; why he was acting like this when merely on a routine official matter. Her secretive mind started firing from all corners to analyze this behavior. Within the next few seconds, her mind established that this macho-man was a softie in front of her and the probable reason would be that he had a certain chemistry toward her. A small 'crush,' so to speak. Her billions of neurons started firing indiscriminately, overwhelming her emotions with a final message of 'I like him.'

"Officer, please come and take a seat." yet again with a

snobbish British Royal accent, which she had acquired over the years.

"Madam, this is the file." He handed over the file and sat down in front of her. She smiled and took the file.

"Give me a few moments just to glance through it."

Ranga felt the necessity for opening a conversion with her.

"Professor, as a matter of fact, you were the one who handed over my PhD certificate at the recent convocation."

Anita just raised her head and looked at him intently, as if she were trying to place him at the event. However, she was actually scrutinizing the male figure right before her, to assess whether this man fulfilled the pre-determined requirements as her future husband. The scanning process lasted only a few seconds, absorbing as much information as was required to conclude whether SSP Ranga fulfilled her desired Lover/Husband characteristics.

With an inquisitive smile, more mysterious than the 'Mona Lisa' herself, "I think I vaguely remember you, because you were the only uniformed student who received a certificate that day, but I cannot recall your height and physique."

At the back of her mind, she thought she could have avoided the last few words. Too late, it was out now! To compensate for this, the very next moment, as women tend to do all the time, she suddenly became serious and professional.

"Officer, I need a few days to study this, you will receive an appointment to see me soon. Thank you very much." Damage control done!

Her body language indicated that Ranga must leave now.

"I'll take your leave, with your permission professor. Please consider this discussion as very private and confidential, since we are not allowed to release such information without a prosecutor's authority. As a matter of fact, I have broken the code of conduct."

"Yes, duly noted!"

With mixed feelings, Ranga left the office.

After the door closed, Anita just sat there with an absolutely blank stare. She had these abrupt mood changes which even her secretive mind was struggling to come to terms with. Outside, she did not want to show her affection toward a male.

However, inside her, she was craving for a man to come and make love to her passionately. She was voluntarily punishing herself to achieve a sense of superiority, which she herself was not sure about. Though this was the case with her love life, regarding the rest of the things like career, family and friends, she was the perfect Human being one could think of.

Ranga got into the Mahindra Police Jeep which was one of the one-thousand jeeps procured by the Department of Police through a credit line received from India. The driver, PC Gnanapala, noticed that the SSP was in deep thought, so he did not want to say anything to distract him.

"Sir, to your office?" No answer. He reversed the vehicle and started driving. "Sorry Gnanapala, yes to my office," a delayed reaction.

Neither talked until they reached their destination.

Upon arrival, Ranga stepped out of the vehicle and walked straight to his office, without even acknowledging the staff.

"What's up with him?" murmured Geetha.

She always wanted to flirt with him and every time he walked past, he used to have eye contact with her in a flirty way or more often than not, make a suggestive remark or two which was his 'throw-away.' Everybody knew about this at the office.

PC Sarath came very close to Geetha, bent over and

whispered in her ear. "That Professor must have given him a hard time," and walked away.

With a sarcastic and knowing smile, she nodded her head and settled down to do whatever she was doing. She was unable to concentrate and her inquisitive mind was throwing a tantrum within her to know what had happened to him.

She couldn't wait any more bottling her desire to inquire as to what had happened, she got up and went toward his closed office door and gently tapped on it.

"Sir, can I bring you a cup of tea?"

She was expecting a big "No." To her pleasant surprise, a gentle and defeated voice said, "Yes, I need one and do you mind coming in?"

She was ecstatic in anticipation! Next second, she was inside his office. This time, no salute!

She looked at him like a lioness with a disabled prey who couldn't run away and with an assumed tender voice, "Sir are you hungry? We brought some tea buns today for tea, if you like I can bring one for you."

Proposition ignored!

"Geetha, expect a call from the Professor any day and as soon as you receive it, let me know."

She was quite annoyed with the reply, since she was anticipating some sort of tender and gentle flirting from him.

"OK sir, I'll bring your tea," and rudely walked out of the office thinking "why should I give him a bun when he is not even contributing to buy these snacks?"

She felt jealous about this professor she had never seen. She thought academics were nerdy and ugly, in an attempt at pacifying her deflated ego.

CHAPTER 5

The red Jaguar turned into the cul-de-sac called 'Ivy Cottage Close,' on Rosemead Place, Colombo seven. It was said that Rosemead place was the most sought-after residential road where many of the elite of Sri Lanka lived. The name Rosemead Place in itself, was a status symbol. This was one of the few surviving names of the British colonial past. Though Ivy Cottage Close was considered a cul-de-sac, there were only two houses in it. True to its name, the perimeter of this area was covered by a 'flagstone,' wall which was constructed with neatly stacked granite and sandstone, probably during the last decade of the eighteenth century. A thick layer of Ivy covered this flagstone wall, leading to the cul-de-sac being named 'Ivy Cottage Close.'

This was the Colombo house of the famous Barrister, George Wickramasooriya.

Anita's mother Helen, never liked to live in Colombo, since she preferred the sedentary and peaceful life at "Wickramasooriya Walauwa," in the hill country. She especially disliked to associate with the snobbish Colombo crowd. Anyway, she left it to her spinster sister-in-law Rose and her husband George, to have the occupancy of the house.

Contrary to her mother's wishes, Anita loved to live in Colombo, also since her work as the Professor of Psychology at the Faculty of Medicine of the University of Colombo, made it more convenient for her to live there.

"Hi Aunty Rose, how is your 'Veranda Lavender,' rose

doing?"

Winding down the manual door glass window, Anita asked her only aunt who lived in the other small house in front and to a side of the main house, situated in Ivy Cottage Close. As a matter of fact, the small house was the office block of the first owner of this property, in late 1800s.

Rose, who was bent over the rose plant, straightened her back. "Not so good dear."

Anita stopped the car and got down. "What's the matter with it?"

"I think it's the mildew, probably powdery mildew, I am not sure."

"Oh dear."

Anita came near the juvenile plant and squatted near it. She didn't have a clue about plants. However, though the Veranda Lavender rose was supposed to be disease resistant; from its appearance, she too noticed that the plant was not looking healthy.

"Aunty, come over for a cup of tea," and drove off toward the main house, which was the private residence of the then Governor of Ceylon, Joseph West Ridgeway, in year 1896.

She pulled the Jaguar into the spacious car port and parked it next to the modified, bright orange colored, Wrangler Jeep. The Jeep was customized with off-road/Rough Country/suspensions, a Dobinson's Snorkel, a nudge bar and a passenger cabin safety bar with four safari lights on top and a powerful Stallion 25,000 lb. winch, which gave it an intimidating look.

On top of the car port, was the 20' X 30' huge room which her late father used as his consulting chambers. Since her father's demise, Anita had converted this huge space as her living quarters, taking advantage of the huge front facing windows.

44

From these windows, she could even observe what was happening right along Rosemead Place.

Her young, live-in maid, Tharanga, upon hearing the car entering the car port, came out to greet her.

"Tharanga, Aunty Rose is coming to have a cup of tea," Tharanga knew the routine.

Aunt Rose, a spinster by choice, was the only sister of her father, who was ten years younger to him. Whilst enjoying a brew of the finest Broken Orange Pekoe tea from high elevation tea estates of Sri Lanka, both of them nibbled at the Scottish vanilla butterscotch biscuits. Rose preferred to dip her biscuits in the tea. Though the initial conversation was about roses and gardening, Rose realized Anita was not her usual self and that her mind was drifting.

"Yes dear, what's bothering you?"

Anita was surprised with this remark, then again, she realized she was not really herself. 'Sherlock Holmes,' Rose, started her cross examination with a leading question,

"Are you in love darling?"

With her cup of tea in her hand, Anita twisted her head toward her aunt; "Why do you ask that?"

"I know dear, you are in love, even though I was never married I have been there."

Anita's rock-solid frozen mind, started to thaw. She just smiled looking at her tea cup and suddenly a juvenile honeybee fell into the tea.

Wet with tea, the honeybee was desperately trying to get out of the cup and swimming awkwardly and aimlessly, looking for a way out.

With its wings wet, the honeybee will never get out of this cup of tea, she thought.

45

Anita's vision conveniently dislodged the sight of the bee and cunningly replaced it with the uniformed Police Officer. He was in the cup, and the honeybee was still trying to escape. Noticing Anita staring at the tea cup, Rose asked,

"Is the tea OK?"

Without saying anything, Anita shouted looking toward the back of the house, "Tharanga, a bee fell into my tea, please bring another cup," and she took another biscuit, broke it in two, dipped one part into the tea and raised the bee out of the tea. She gently kept the piece of biscuit on the saucer. Though the bee started to drag its feet and move, it was not able to fly away, probably due to the stickiness of the sugar in the tea.

Is this me? she thought. Then her thought process was rudely interrupted, "So, tell me dear, I am all ears!"

Anita poured another tea into the fresh cup brought by her maid. She stirred in a tea spoonful of sugar and kept the spoon out on the saucer. Then she noticed the bee still struggling without much success. She took a small sip of tea and kept the cup on the saucer;

"Aunty, I just met this young and handsome Police SSP today."

"OK, go on."

"I think he is interested in me."

Breaking her promise of 'all ears,' Rose interrupted,

"Can I re-phrase it like this? – I am interested in him," with a rather sarcastic though sweet smile. Anita, even without looking at her aunt, whilst looking at the still struggling bee, just smiled.

"My dear Anita duwa (daughter), go for him!"

She swallowed the last bit of the Butterscotch biscuit and washed it down with the remaining tea.

"I've got to water the plants, thank you for the tea, I like the vanilla butterscotch," and Rose got up and left.

Anita watched her dear aunt walking toward her flower patch with a blank face. However, from the corner of her eye, she could see the honeybee still trying a valiant attempt to free itself from the trap it got itself into.

"No, you are well and truly stuck mate, soon a gecko or a spider is going to eat you alive." with this somewhat cruel thought, she got up and left.

As soon as she reached the stairway leading to her personal abode upstairs, she changed her mind, went to the kitchen and got some tap water into a spoon. She carried it carefully to the honeybee and poured it over him, hoping the water might dilute the effect of the stickiness, so the bee could free itself.

"OK mate this is all I can do, best of luck," and left.

From her upstairs window, Anita looked at the front view and she saw her Aunt Rose tending to her precious plants. Just the thought of her aunt being a spinster, had haunted her mind for many years. She thought Rose would have been a 'dashy,' catch in her prime! To end up like this not being married, brought frightful imaginations to her tender, yet stereotype mind. She saw herself, tending to the flower plants thirty years from now.

Though she was not really superstitious, she thought she should go and see the bee. Without even changing her clothes, she came back to where the bee was. It was not to be seen. She was not sure, if it was eaten or had flown away to its much-desired freedom, either to repeat the same mistake or to avoid doing it again.

She had a shower and came out of the bathroom stark naked, the daily routine she was used to. Her Bang & Olufsen stereo was crying 'play me, play me'.

She couldn't resist the cry. "OK, okay, be patient," she warned the stereo and walked toward the huge ebony almirah with intricate carvings. She couldn't resist wearing her 'Bonsoir' night shirt just on its own.

The smooth silk was caressing her body lightly, whilst her partially wet body tried to grab the garment with the intention of not letting it go. Her prominent nipples managed to cling on to the Bonsoir silk as if that were part of her body.

Her Bang & Olufsen was a late 1970s cabinet type record player.

"OK grumpy, what do you like to play? Is Elvis good enough for you or do you want Wild Cherry's 'Play that Funky Music'? I see, you are in a bad mood. So, lets funky."

She inserted the EP, pressed the play button and went toward the coconut wood liquor trolley with two large non-rotating wheels. A half empty Remy Martin Louis XIII bottle of Champagne Cognac was smiling at her.

"OK girl, I am yours!"

From the lower shelf, she took a Bohemian Crystal snifter and poured a stiff drink. Cradling the snifter in her cupped tender palm, in between the middle and the fourth finger, she sniffed the aroma of the heavenly liquid.

The snifter was craving for her sweet lips. Nodding her head with an approving gesture, she obliged the snifter. She retained the brandy in her mouth for a few seconds to let the taste buds achieve their anticipated ecstasy. Then she swallowed it slowly and whilst the fine quality liquor was finding its way to her stomach, she reached 'Mr. Grumpy.'

To her amazement, grumpy was not grumpy anymore and was 'funking,' with the music of Wild Cherry. Quickly finding its way to her brain, the alcohol was inspiring her to increase the volume of 'not so grumpy,' to near maximum. Nearly 150 of RMS vibrated the base speaker, shedding its dust like a dog out of the water. The 50 HZ base frequency, with a 70 dB sound volume, synchronized the teak wooden upper floor in unison with the Bang & Olufsen, playing the 'funky,' music.

A few sips of the Cognac and 'Once I was a boogie singer,' lyrics couldn't restrict the young cougar to stay sedentary.

She darted out of her favorite 'Beecher,' genuine leather reclining chair and started dancing away in a frenzied yet rhythmic trance, reminiscing her wild late teens. Whilst dancing and still maintaining the funky rhythm, she went near the huge front windows and drew the voile net curtain, slowly.

She very well knew that due to the interior lights, one could see the shadow from outside and her inner mind wished for prying eyes, giving her sexuality a welcome boost!

CHAPTER 6

SSP Ranga Fernando opened the sealed, somewhat fat file, which was sent to him by the DIG Central Province office through the police department's 'secured special delivery system.'

He rang the desk top bell. The very next instant, eternally hopeful WPC Geetha, peeped through the slightly opened door.

Only her face was visible "Sir, you called?" anticipating SSP Ranga would ask her to come into the office.

"Geetha, please don't disturb me, no calls, no visitors, until I tell you."

"Yes Sir," disappointed, Geetha answered her superior officer and closed the door heavily, making an unpleasant sound.

She heard the SSP's muffled voice, "Thank you, Geetha," through the closed door. The file contained photocopies of various documents certified by the Central DIG's office. Police reports, crime scene photos, the post-mortem report and various other investigation reports.

He didn't know where to begin, even though he was usually very good at analyzing these. He was more concerned about the JMO's report. He glanced through it hoping to discover the ghastly nature of this despicable murder. However, the JMO's professional opinion was contrary to his expectations.

His bewildering information was 'There was no evidence to suggest any sexual molestation whatsoever.'

He was stunned! The JMO appeared quite confident about

this piece of information. He read the same thing over and over again very slowly and kept on reading it very attentively.

The cause of death was due to a fracture-dislocation of the Axis (second cervical vertebrae) and Atlas (first cervical vertebrae), probably due to forceful and violent twisting of the head, causing the transection of the spinal cord completely. Further to that, cervical vertebrae three, four and five displaying rotational fractures with massive hematoma in the para cervical vertebral space, were found. The right carotid artery was severed at the cervical two, three and four vertebrae levels. This could be the reason for the massive hematoma found.

No evidence of sexual molestation found? Ranga was flummoxed!

Though Ranga couldn't understand the medical jargon, the message was clear. This child died of violent twisting of the head. It sounded really morbid!

That thought brought back the 'Special Crime Prevention,' lectures he had attended and the self-defense training, he had undergone at the police Commando Unit, during his SI days as a young police officer. In unarmed combat, one of the methods taught in stealthily neutralizing the enemy, was twisting the head of the opponent.

Ranga did not bother to read anything else and something told him, "Come on man, this is your opportunity to pursue your desire – yes, Anita time!"

In this instance, he did not want to ask Geetha to make the appointment. He picked up his mobile and rang Prof. Anita's office personal direct line. The phone started ringing.

He could feel that he was nervous, and noticed a very fine shake of his hand and felt his mouth getting dry. He cleared his

51

throat, anticipating Anita's voice. It felt like an eternity before the call was answered, though it was only after five rings. However, adding to his chagrin, the call was directed to the answering machine.

"Hello, this is Professor Anita Wickramasooriya, right now I am not available to answer your call personally, please leave your name, telephone number and inquiry subject after the tone."

'Bloody answering machines,' annoyed, Ranga said to himself.

"Hello professor, this is SSP Ranga, I received the murder report docket, and I wish to discuss this with you in person, if and when convenient to you. Thank you professor." He hung up, much relieved.

Then he started reading through the other documents.

Anita came to her office after finishing her lecture at the medical faculty. As soon as she entered, she saw the flashing green LED light in the desk top phone. In comes Jine.

"Jine, I need a coffee please."

"OK madam, can I make a cup of your Aunt Rose's coffee?"

"Yes please."

Then she pressed the message button. When she heard the SSP's voice, her first impression was that the tone reflected a disappointed person's voice.

Her own thought process was fighting within, "Am I going to answer him now or am I deliberately going to delay it?"

However, the passion of anticipated love won the battle of 'ego versus love, 'by a huge margin!

It was the SSP's personal mobile number. 'Yes, he wants me to have his number.' In a somewhat elated mood and an action orientated mind; 'I am going to ring him with my personal mobile number.'

When she was about to punch the number, she changed her mind, as any women would have done. 'Changing her mind is a woman's privilege' they say. No certainly not!' Ego versus passion at loggerheads.

'I am not cheap and easy! Compromise, compromise girl,' 'OK, I am going to send him a text.' Her mind was in a tangle!

'Dear Officer Fernando, this is to inform you that I shall be available from twelve noon to four p.m. at the Dept. of Psychology.' She didn't want to compromise her standard. However, she had already saved his number as 'SSP Ranga.'

Jinadasa brought the aroma-emitting coffee in her favorite mug which was also given to her by Aunt Rose. She placed the mobile on her desk and just tasted the first sip of this finest coffee. She glanced at the Cartier watch she was wearing. The time was 11.55 a.m. She just started to enjoy the coffee by retaining every sip inside her mouth for a few seconds, so her taste buds had the time to adsorb it.

Sharp at twelve noon, the mobile rang. While she was holding the mug in her right hand and bringing it to her mouth to have the next sip, Anita glanced at the mobile. It was Ranga who was ringing without sending a text in reply. Whilst grabbing the mobile with her left hand, she kept the mug on the desk. In her excitement, she toppled the coffee mug completely on to the desk and the coffee started dripping from the edge of the desk onto the Calvin Klein dress pants she was wearing.

She had already pressed the answer button and instead of saying "Hello", "Oh shit!" a spontaneous outburst sprang out of her mouth. To avoid the dripping coffee, she got up from her chair and quite embarrassed, said,

"Sorry Officer Ranga, I tend to spill coffee every time you

ring me, my apologies for using bad language."

That was the opening Ranga was craving for, to break the barrier. "Am I that bad Professor, do I scare you?"

"Oh no, not at all! I tend to be clumsy sometimes" rather matter-of-factly.

Both of them thought they had broken down the barriers of ego, dominance and fear. However, each one decided 'I am going to play it safe.'

"Professor you need to see these reports."

"I am available now onwards; you are most welcome to visit our department."

Anita made sure to keep the conversation somewhat official, without giving away too much of her inner feelings.

Ranga was there within no time, so Anita guessed that he was already on his way when he rang her. Ranga entered Anita's office and saluted her after placing his hat between the left upper arm and the side of his chest.

"Officer, do you drive a Ferrari?" sarcasm at its best!

It took a few split seconds for Ranga to grasp the meaning and to defend himself "No ma'am, I fly!" with equal sarcasm.

Both of them laughed, implying they had reached the same path of communication. Anita took the documents and started reading the JMO's report. Ranga could see her eyes getting bigger and smaller alternately and the wrinkling of her forehead from time to time.

"Professor, the aroma of the coffee is tempting and it's a crime to spill it," "Would you like one?"

"As a matter of fact, I'd love to"

Anita called Jine and asked him to make more coffee. "Jine, I also need one please, I spilled mine." and looked straight at Ranga with penetrating eyes, implying he was to be blamed.

"This is bizarre! We are looking at a different level psychopath, good subject for an MSc." She deviated the whole conversation more toward professionalism.

"Professor, what are we looking at?" It was just a line to start a conversation on Ranga's part. "Officer, this personality could be anyone, even a female," came the reply.

With raised eyebrows, Ranga looked through Anita; "Even a woman eh? What makes you to say that?"

"The victim is a child, so even a woman can inflict such an injury." Ranga knew there was nothing to go on, so he made use of his charm and ingenuity to maintain the rapport between them.

"Madam, I was just wondering if it is okay to ask you something completely unrelated."

Anita was expecting something of that nature to keep the conversation going but nevertheless, acted surprised, "Yes, officer."

"As you know, in relation to my PhD, I would like to continue doing my research, and I have reason to believe our department is going to name me as the representative to attend the UN Global Crime Prevention Forum in Geneva next year." He paused.

"Do you think you can provide me guidance and coach me to write and read a paper at this Forum? Perhaps you can come up with a relevant topic."

Anita pretended that she was merely trying her best to help him. However, inside her, emotions were running wild and in an uncontrollable frenzy, thought, 'I am going to nail it now!'

"Why not we meet to discuss this in detail one of these days?"

"Professor, that would be nice, can you suggest a day please?"

"Are you free this Friday evening?"

Without beating round the bush, Anita made the first move. "Yes."

"Six p.m., Golf Club"

"OK ma'am." Ranga got up, took one step back and saluted her wholeheartedly. He was on cloud nine while returning to his office.

CHAPTER 7

"Edward, please let go of that innocent frog!"

Josephina shouted at her second son Edward who was just five years old, when she saw him holding a huge green frog. The frog was desperately trying to escape from Edward's grip and succeeded for a brief moment.

The frog took a long leap with a frightened croak. After the second leap, the frog was almost six feet away from the little boy. However, Edward was fast and sleek and he literally dived at the frog like an eagle, landing on the grass and grabbing it with both hands. Josephina was amazed by her son's reflexes, and thought he would be a fine rugby player one day.

She was amazed and couldn't believe her own eyes at what happened afterwards, as her dreams were shattered!

Edward grabbed the frog's body very tightly with his left hand and grasped the head with his right; and in an instant, twisted the head completely around, causing both its eyes to pop out like corks from champagne bottles.

He brought the lifeless carcass near his face and twisted the mangled head further. Its white tongue appeared from nowhere, making a frightful sight. He then brought the dead frog close to his face.

"You slimy animal, you deserve to die."

He laughed and tossed it into air and kicked the dead body over the flowering hedge.

Josephina felt dizzy and sat on the steps from where she

was watching this despicable act unfolding right before her eyes. Later that day, when her husband Stanislaus came home from his estate inspection round, Josephina did not even wait for him to have his cup of tea.

"Stan darling, something terrible happened today." "Yes Jozi, tell me what happened."

She described the incident. Stan did not say anything initially, "Is this the first time?" "Something ghastly as this? Yes."

Stan embraced a deep thought of his own and looked at Jozi with a puzzled look. "What's wrong darling, why are you looking at me like that?" asked Jozi.

"No nothing, he is not like George."

Jozi looked at her husband with a questioning look but did not say anything. "George is just like me." One could see Jozi was getting annoyed.

"What are you implying Stan?" Jozi shot back in a somewhat raised tone.

"What I meant to say was, George is just like me, but Edward is completely different," Annoyed, Jozi left her husband without uttering a word.

This was the second time a dark cloud engulfed the marriage of Josephina and Stanislaus.

Stan took out his Whitluck's Tobacco Pipe and started clearing the remnant tobacco inside the pipe's chamber. This was his favorite act when he felt nervous and upset.

He was looking at the pipe chamber and his mind was drifting away with a feeling of trepidation; due to the rumors which were circulating those days at the turf club, when Edward was born. Inside the chamber, he even visualized the prominent nose of the 'baby Edward,' when he was born. Quite unintentionally, he touched his rather flat nose and continued scraping the chamber which was by now, devoid of any tobacco residue.

Angrily he got up, leaving the pipe on a stool. He went toward the room which both George and Edward shared.

Both of them were playing happily and his anger disappeared instantly. George was trying to hug his little brother.

However, Edward was pushing him away screaming,

"Mommy, Aiya *(older brother)* is trying to hug me." at the top of his voice. Stan turned back to see Jozi standing right behind him just a few inches away, with an angry and worried face. Stan left the area as if nothing had happened.

"George let go of Malli *(younger brother)*. Both of you come with me," Josephina tactfully diverted the attention of her two sons.

"Come, I am going to make a hot chocolate drink, who wants it?"

"Me, me," both screamed in unison and followed their mother to the kitchen.

That day, a 'healed wound,' was reopened, to turn into a 'pus oozing,' ugly carbuncle.

Months passed without any further incidents. However, the thick cloud of suspicion and betrayal never improved between Stan and Jozi. One fine morning, their domestic help came running with a frightened face, "Madam, our cat is dead!"

Jozi knew instinctively what it was and did not want to go anywhere near it or even to look at it.

"Can you bury it before anyone sees it?"

The domestic help was surprised with this unusual request, since both her madam and the elder son George, loved the cat immensely. This behavior puzzled her and she was at a loss for words.

However, Stan was inquisitive and came almost running, "Where is it?" "Corridor near the kitchen sir."

He was horrified to see the lifeless body of the lovable cat lying with its head twisted 180 degrees and its tongue coming out like a tiny spade.

He couldn't bear the sight, even though he was a veteran hunter. He did not want to show any emotions.

"Can you please bury it before the children get up? Make sure you do not mention it to anyone. We will say the cat has gone missing."

The domestic help was nonplussed but both Stan and Jozi knew instantly what would have happened to the cat. However, their ways of thinking about the predicament they had to encounter, were miles apart.

Stan was angry and furious at himself because he assumed that his 'uppish' behavior and aristocratic ego, had led to this situation and now he felt beyond any doubt, that Edward was not his child!

He got into his jungle khaki planter's trousers and Polo neck long sleeved T shirt; put on his rather worn-out, Akubra Balmoral planters' hat, his favorite Aldo travel boots and picked up his simple cane walking stick. This time, he optimally packed his pipe with Virginia tobacco and lit it with his vintage 'grinding wheel,' flint, brass kerosene lighter.

Stan had to get out of the house to think and formulate his plan on how to overcome this storm.

However, Jozi was in a pensive mood with tears dripping slowly down her cheeks, regretting her actions of a few years back. She felt sad that she had betrayed a good man and she knew these things could not be undone, ever! It was not a simple 'heat of the moment,' incident. It had been meticulously planned and secretly executed; and which one could refer to as 'the mother of all betrayals'!

She was feeling ashamed of herself and hated her own body and soul. Since that day, neither one of them had brought up that subject nor tried to solve the crisis. Jozi became very silent and private.

However, she became more protective of Edward with every trivial incident that ensued over the years.

Contrary to this, Stan became more dominant and started implementing stringent rules in the 'Wickramasooriya,' mansion, though he imposed no undue strictness toward George. This was mainly because he was always well behaved and obliging.

However, both of them were treated with the same love and care. This attitude pacified Jozi into believing that she was married to a real 'Gentleman,' and was happy to be 'the Mrs. Wickramasooriya.'

A year later, an unexpected event took place, when the couple were blessed with a pretty, bouncy baby girl who was bestowed the name Rosy.

The two boys grew up happy and protected, though the sudden and bizarre deaths of animals with twisted necks, continued from time to time. Chickens, squirrels and small amphibians, were the usual victims within the vast estate, except on one instance, when a fully grown goat met with a similar fate. The goat belonged to an estate worker. The whole estate was puzzled as to how this strong goat met with such an inexplicable death.

Various theories circulated amongst the whole work force but only the Wickramasooriyas and the mansion staff, knew the exact truth. Loyal servants of the mansion dared not speak about it. Perhaps the colonial mind-set of the mansion staff and the handsome bonuses they received, kept the lid on these ugly incidents.

A privilege enjoyed by the 'high society,' of Sri Lanka in general.

In the meantime, Rose, the little baby girl, was growing up to be a treat and a handful, keeping the mother and the staff quite busy and entertained.

Years passed by without much ado. A few skirmishes with the schoolmates every now and then, regular bizarre and mysterious deaths of various small animals, always with twisted heads; was the order of the day. The near and dear to the Wickramasooriyas, got used to this and conditioned themselves as if they were normal happenings.

Edward and his elder brother George, attended the school nearby. Due to Edward's unusual behavior, children christened him as "smarty weirdo," and it was established permanently, replacing his name. Edward himself was proud of it and took advantage of such terminology to subdue other kids; and no one dared to challenge him.

However, George's fortunes were not that 'Rosy' as far as typical boy's behavior was concerned. Since George was mild in temperament and quite tolerant, he was subject to light hearted teasing by his mates and at numerous times, 'Smarty Weirdo,' had to intervene and rescue his elder brother.

Their school was situated just a walking distance from the estate. Both brothers used to take a short cut through their estate, which a few of the other students also used. At the edge of the estate where the school perimeter fence was located, there was an area with a few tall boulders, a steep slope and a narrow footpath, used by the students to reach the school. The students used this route every day.

It was a Friday afternoon, after school, a few students including the 'Wickramasooriya,' brothers were walking home. As usual, Edward was walking behind the others, since he always preferred to walk alone. George was with two other boys in front, and they were in a boisterous mood thinking about the weekend. No one seemed to notice Edward who was walking behind them.

Out of them, the tallest boy Thusith was making fun of George;

"Hey you sissy, can I bring you a skirt to wear?" and pushed him in fun.

George fell down and was struggling to get up. Seeing his brother being bullied, Edward darted toward Thusith, shouting,

"You 'sonofobicth,' this is the last time you are doing it!"

Thusith did not have time to react. Edward, who was smaller and shorter than Thusith jumped up, grabbed his head with both hands and twisted it like a bottle cap, rotating it nearly 360 degrees. It was instant!

The big boy's flaccid body dropped like a log. His tongue was out and his eyes were wide open. The other two boys were stunned and couldn't speak! It all happened in an instant and they had no time to intervene.

Probably, their survival instincts would have kicked in and they opted for 'flight,' abandoning the 'fight,' component of the famous 'Fight or Flight,' phenomenon.

Thusith was stone dead by the time he hit the ground on the narrow pathway in between two huge boulders, with his neck twisted! George was still down, watching the drama in horror, unable to fathom what was happening.

The next moment, Edward dragged the lifeless body on to the somewhat flat boulder with some difficultly and pushed it over saying,

"You deserve to die, you low animal," and spat.

The body fell with a loud thud on to another boulder about 10 meters down below, cracking the skull! He came toward his brother who was watching all this but still struggling to stand up due to his legs having gone flaccid at witnessing this horrific sight!

Edward came up to him and helped him to stand up. "Not a word," and ran away. In the confusion, George forgot his school bag and started walking like a zombie toward home.

Somehow, the coroner's verdict was vague as to the cause of death and the police eventually reported that the missing boy was nowhere to be found. The parents of the victim were said to have been handsomely compensated and it was declared an 'open and shut,' case, as it was clear that there was no real evidence to proceed with it.

CHAPTER 8

Anita came walking with a slinky movement in front of her 3' by 6' mirror, wearing her Chanel Cruise collection long skirt and a matching sleeveless blouse, then turned round mimicking the catwalk. Her eyes were glued on the mirror, and she was very pleased with her figure. She knew she had already bagged her trophy and her only desire was to keep it only for herself.

"Grumpy, please play something nice." Anita knew grumpy would never disappoint her. "Grumpy, which perfume will seduce this hunk, is it Black Opium or Poison?"

"OK, I heard it, it's Opium then"

By this time, grumpy was playing Lulu's 'I'm a Tiger' and Anita the tigress was ready for her kill, with Chanel and Opium.

'No mercy,' she thought. By way of insurance, she took her Gucci hand bag and Cartier wrist watch. That was a formidable outfit!

However, with her feminine figure and the inviting smile, she simply did not really need any one of this materialistic paraphernalia. Probably the order of the day would have been 'Just the way you are.'

When she came out of the house, "Hello dear, aren't we going hunting?"

Aunt Rose just happened to be standing near her Jaguar.

"Good luck darling, don't torture him too much! You know these rugged looking guys are really fragile, so handle with care," and she winked at her and walked toward her abode, waving without even looking at her.

It was normally only a few minutes' drive to the Royal Colombo Golf Club, but the city traffic was not too kind to her. Since it was a Friday, the car park was almost full by the time she reached her destination. When she found a spot to park the beast, she heard a rather noisy motorcycle approaching the car park, as if it were about to explode!

'Who is this imbecile riding a motorbike with a busted exhaust?' she thought, as she was locking the car. The very next moment there he was, wearing a white Crocodile Polo shirt, a faded ragged denim and an immaculately shiny pair of brown laced Clarks shoes.

He was riding a noisy 1958 Harley-Davidson Duo-Glide, obviously with a leaking exhaust! "Officer, is there any law in this country against noise pollution?"

"I am the law!"

Ranga got down from the saddle and switched off the engine. "Have you ever heard there is something called welding?"

"But, I like a noisy entrance."

"Hope you live up to your reputation of noisy things!"

Ranga just froze! In the fading light of the setting sun, the silhouette of her shapely figure against the faintly illuminating car park light, mesmerized him; creating mayhem in his mind, thinking whether he was visualizing an angel! She was a far cry from the professor, he had seen earlier! He was stunned and his voice was lost. His mind was busy trying to grasp the dazzling beauty right before his own eyes, abandoning his vocal cords.

He was speechless!

"Careful, your jaw might drop off, come on, I am dying for a drink."

Anita walked toward the entrance and registered with the

facial recognition scanner. After signing her guest in, she walked toward the verandah facing the 16th hole.

It was a spectacular sight! The time was ten minutes past six. She sat facing the Golf course. Instead of sign language, she used her sparkling eyes to guide him. Ranga followed her like a poodle following his mistress and sat on the chair opposite her; where apart from observing the unbelievably beautiful specimen of a female in his full gaze, nothing else was there to be visualized. Ranga didn't mind, because his attention was entirely focused on Anita alone! He was not there to enjoy the sunset.

"Professor, what would you like to have?"

The waiter who was wearing black trousers and a white short sleeved shirt, asked Anita and looked at Ranga anticipating his order as well.

"Brad, the usual for me."

Bradley the waiter, looked at Ranga.

"I'll have a single malt on the rocks thank you."

"Brad, we also need cashew, potato wedges and hot butter cuttlefish."

Anita had a hearty look at the male specimen before her and promised herself, 'I am not going to let him go'!

"So, professor, I am intrigued about your usual. Is it something psychologists drink or something big-time professors' drink?"

"Oh no, it's good old gin and tonic with ample ice, of course, with a slice of lemon and a spearmint garnish; and for the last time, please don't call me professor, you can call me Anita!" A dazzling smile!

Anita felt very relaxed in his presence. However, Ranga was miles away, debating within himself whether he was doing the right thing or getting into a bottomless wormhole, to get lost.

67

A debate where humble vs elite backgrounds were at loggerheads with each other; with each side winning and losing alternately, was churning within his mind.

However, the clear winner was the alcohol which bulldozed both sides of the argument, just after it reached the 200 ml mark. So, it was 'winner takes all,' and the alcohol was well on the way to being the clear winner! Anita of course was calm and maintaining her cool throughout. When the 5th order was placed, Anita picked up her mobile and ordered an 'Uber,' cab. Ranga was trying to keep up with the watering capacity and speed of Anita, making sure of neither over-watering nor spilling the can.

"OK noisy one, let's go and put you to the test."
She got up, signed the bill and handed it over to Brad, with a handsome tip. Ranga was bewildered as to what was happening, and just decided the best bet was to follow her regardless. She was looking at the mobile while talking to herself and said, "three minutes." By that time, the single malt was hitting him like an eighteen-wheeler! Yet he managed to walk without staggering.

Anita was steady, just like her beast! "OK our transport is here."

On the portico, the Uber Prius was waiting. "Get in." Ranga just saved his life by opening the door for her,

"Oh, you are such a gentleman, thank you," adding an extra vowel into the thank you. Her voice was steady and her speech was not slurring. The multiple G & Ts had nothing on her!

"Driver, 'Cloud 9'," the driver just nodded.

'Cloud 9' disco was situated on the top floor of a high-rise building. The Main entrance at the ground floor, was guarded by huge, fierce looking bouncers with no visible necks. The meanest looking one stopped Ranga.

"Oh, he is with me." To his surprise, this giant just stepped aside and saluted Anita.

The top floor was a completely different world! Noise, laser lights, holograms, multi-colored smoke; and above all, a kind of weird techno music, which Ranga had never even heard of.

Young waiters, both boys and girls wearing hot pants, braces and shirtless, served the equally weird young and old customers. Ranga was at a loss for words but pretended he loved the place. He could smell the cannabis and just wondered what would happen if there was a raid by the police.

Anita ordered more gin and tonic for both of them and Ranga willingly obliged. Some eerie music started and Anita went into a frenzy, dragging hapless Ranga on to the floor packed with a writhing mass of humans. Various illegal substances appeared from nowhere and Ranga couldn't resist any as a 'first timer.'

So, he stuck to the old proverb "When in Rome, do as the Romans do!"

He did not have any recollection of what happened after that, yet he remembered Anita's energy of non-stop dancing. That's the day he lost the concept of time!

The next thing he remembered was, "Come on darling, take a shower with me."

There she was completely naked, inside the tempered glass shower cubicle, caressing her hair upwards, with the shower forming a running mist. Ranga was in a trance. Only then did he realize he was also naked.

"Can you live up to your noisy entrance?"

CHAPTER 9

After the death of her beloved husband, George, Helen felt her life was not worth living. Spiritually and emotionally, she was ready to depart this world and had forgiven herself for the sins she had committed throughout her life.

However, her mind was not at complete peace, since Anita was still single. Inside of her, she knew Anita was headstrong and capable of looking after her own life. However, the management of this vast wealth bothered her since there was no other heir. It was a mega task which she thought Anita couldn't take on single-handedly.

It was Saturday morning, and she was getting rather apprehensive. She thought "I can't wait until Sunday morning to ring Anita as usual."

Helen never had a mobile telephone, and there was no necessity for her to have one either, since she hardly ever ventured out of their estate.

Helen dialed on the 'rotating number,' dial plate of the antique telephone. The clicks for each numerical digit made a soothing sound which filled one's auditory system; indicating that actually physically, something was happening to help one to talk to ones loved one, in comparison with digitally different tones. The time lapse for each digit to register and the number of clicks, brings confidence to the person who is dialing on an ancient telephone.

Anita's mobile started ringing.

Two naked bodies, cuddled up together forming a bizarre arrangement of body parts, was a novel scene to Grumpy who always stood silent and stationary, close to the massive mirror; until such time he was opted into satiating Anita's hunger for music and dancing!

Unfortunately, grumpy could neither describe nor express the strange things which happened right in front of him in the last twelve hours. Grumpy would have murdered the person who said "Walls have ears," if it were alive. There would have been a riot if the mirror, the wardrobe, the wooden ceiling and Grumpy, were all alive!

Something like this had never happened inside Ivy Cottage in its two-hundred-year history. Such intense, passionate and wild, love making!

One could have said "Only if this ceiling could speak," and would have written a brand-new chapter called 'Never Seen Before,' for the ancient 'Kamasutra.'

Anita was fast asleep keeping her head on the upper chest of Ranga who was awake, though suffering from a spitting headache and a loss of time and space. He simply didn't know where he was and how he got there.

However, he was pleased to see a woman cuddling up to him and he did not want to let her go. Anita's left arm was across his chest and her bent left leg was partially covering his lower abdomen. Her grip was so tight that he was virtually a prisoner of Anita's, which he was of course, proud of. A crumpled thin white sheet was entangled between their bodies in awkward places.

"Anita, wake up, your phone is ringing."

Not even a *hmmm*! He shook her once gently. No response. She appeared completely spaced out! He just couldn't locate the phone. After about ten rings, it stopped.

Then he saw her sweet and innocent looking face, resting peacefully in his arms. At that point, his lust took a dramatic turn and he felt something was happening to him; a strange feeling he had never experienced in his whole life, which he couldn't explain himself.

His frigid heart started melting and the paradigm of his way of thinking about women shifted completely. He looked at the ceiling allowing his school of thought to burst through it and he started floating in silk, flowers and babies; and imagined his mother's voice calling out to him. "Don't hurt little girls." He was thoroughly enjoying it when the phone rang again.

Helen was worried since Anita didn't answer the phone the first time. Just then, the Grandfather's clock chimed ten times. She could hear the phone ringing at the other end.

This time, Ranga shook her vigorously and gently took her arm off him. However, the grip of her leg was solid, reminding him of the WWE super-star leg locks, which he enjoyed watching immensely. Her head was still resting on his chest and she started mumbling something which he couldn't grasp. Then all of a sudden she relaxed her leg grip and turned around 180 degrees, freeing Ranga in the process. He sat up on the bed and got out of it.

Then he saw Anita's ringing mobile showing '*Ammi*.' He immediately came round the other side of the bed still naked and sat beside her saying, "Hey, Anita, it is your mom."

By this time, she was wide awake.

"Darling, tell her I'll ring tonight." Ranga was not sure whether he shoulder answer or not.

"Come on you big boy, she is not going to eat you!" and she

turned completely on her stomach   exposing her shapely round buttocks and hourglass shaped waist and hips. For a few microseconds, Ranga enjoyed her delectable figure and with his eyes still glued on her,

"Are you sure?"

"Yees," with an extra vowel and covered her head completely with a pillow.

Hesitantly, Ranga tapped the answer button and stood up "She is sleeping still, and she said she will ring you tonight."

"You will look after her won't you?" and Helen hung up.

Ranga was pleasantly surprised and started thinking. Anita's mother hadn't bothered to ask him who he was or his name.

However, he felt he belonged here and something told him that now he definitely had a responsibility to look after her.

He kept the phone on the bedside stool and realized he was still naked. All this time, he was acting like a robot and suddenly he realized he was with the professor on a 'binge,' and he had a wild night he had never experienced before!

He looked again at Anita. She was sleeping with the pillow over her head. Suddenly, he smelt his own dried-up sweat, after a really crazy night which he couldn't remember much of. After picking up his underwear, trousers and his polo shirt scattered all over, with his left hand, he walked to the bathroom still naked. Near the door, there was a rack with open shelves stacked with bathrobes, bath towels, face towels and hand towels. He took a bathrobe and left the door ajar.

The warm and powerful shower was soothing to his skin and he took the liberty of using Anita's 'flowery fragrance,' foreign soap, shampoo and strong mint toothpaste which he rubbed on his teeth with his finger. Having revitalized his body and soul, he stepped out of the shower wrapping the bathrobe around his waist. He felt that his headache was somewhat better now.

He collected Anita's clothes which were also spread all over the room like a bomb blast site and carefully put them into the dirty linen hamper.

He sat beside Anita and there she was, still sleeping like a log face down, with her head covered with the pillow and nothing else. Then he heard a gentle tap on the door, "Madam, I have made breakfast for two, I am leaving the tray outside." Ranga heard the receding footsteps and then complete silence.

He could smell the aroma of coffee which he had experienced before at her office. He slightly opened the door which was not locked all this time and peeped outside. No one was to be seen. He picked up the tray and kept it on the little ebony table with intricate carvings, facing the window. There were four matching ebony chairs.

He went toward his sleeping beauty and remembered only a kiss would awaken a 'sleeping beauty.' Kissing the lips was not possible so he kissed her shoulder gently. A muffled voice emanated from underneath the pillow, "Pour me a coffee will you?"

Then she got up and walked straight to the bathroom, even without closing the door. Ranga poured out two cups and started sipping one. He heard the flushing of the toilet and then the shower splashing, "Can you come and rub this body wash on my back please?" The coffee be damned!

He was still in a trance and remembered mumbling 'Your wish is my command.' As soon as he went in, she pulled the bathrobe off him and dragged him into the shower cubicle; handed him the body wash lotion and turned her back toward him, with the water still running continuously.

The jasmine fragrance filled his nostrils, and he could see streaks of water with bubbles running down her shapely body as if they were cleansing her body and soul in one go!

She turned toward him and asked him to continue applying the body wash. He was wondering how she had body wash rubbed on her all these days. Then suddenly, she put her arms over his shoulders and locked her fingers around his neck. Even before he realized it, she jumped up and wrapped her thighs round his waist and locked her ankles behind him. Her grip was so tight and solid, like a rivet!

He reached the zenith of arousal! What transpired next would really be forbidden to an audience below eighteen years of age. However, it does not imply that under-eighteens refrain from relishing such pleasurable moments!

At the other end, Helen was ecstatic; she felt as if she was in some kind of heaven and had got rid of the huge weight on her back. All these years, she thought Anita was not interested in men, as she had never even spoken about a man ever since her return from England. She was worried that Anita might end up a spinster like her Aunt Rose.

"Ensa, can you send a message to Tudor to come immediately, I want to go to 'Dalada Maligawa,' (*the Temple of the Tooth*)."

Tudor was the long-standing family chauffeur who was driving the 'Wickramasooriya Walauwa,' vehicles. He lived on a part of the estate where faithful servants were given their own freehold property to live in, usually after fifteen years of loyal and faithful service.

She was over the moon! She found a new energy, she never thought she had in herself and walked up to the Jasmine flower bush which was covered with layers of flowers, like a coating of newly fallen snow.

She took the little cane basket she had got made especially for this purpose, from 'Wewaldeniya,' the village of cane weavers, according to her own design. Every morning without fail, she would offer flowers to Lord Buddha and light the clay, coconut oil lamp.

The shrine was tailor made with white marble, erected by her husband's father Stan, long years ago. After picking about fifteen pure fresh flowers gently, taking care not to squash them; she sprinkled a little pure water she had obtained from the natural spring water pipe, which kept flowing continuously and found its way to the stream below.

Today, she had all the reasons to show Lord Buddha who preached about life, of which probably even five percent was not understood by many people; her gratitude for showing her the precepts that patience, acceptance and being non-judgmental, will have its own merits one day.

In her heart, she wanted to show her gratitude to Lord Buddha; and resolved that the 'Temple of the Tooth,' or 'Dalada Maligawa,' as the local's referred to; was the most venerable shrine in Sri Lanka to pay homage to this greatest of teachers.

After breakfast, both of them hit the bed again since the aftereffects of last night's alcohol and other substances, were still circulating in their bodies making them feel heavy-headed. After completing their 'unfinished business,' Ranga wrapped himself with a white bed sheet, and Anita got into her 'Paddington Bear,' pajamas, feeling completely satiated.

It was only around five p.m. that both of them came back to their normal selves and realized the Jaguar and the Harley-Davidson were still parked at the Golf Club. Anita rang the club and informed them that they would be collecting them on Sunday.

Whilst all these pleasurable things were happening behind drawn curtains, someone with a pair of eagle eyes and highly inquisitive mind, was suffering immensely, wanting to know what was going on! Rose!

In the morning, she did her 'reconnaissance,' mission to try and get a glimpse of the hunk that ventured into Anita's room; around six a.m. and again around five p.m., when she smelled they were up. She hated the opaque Damask curtain material which was hung covering the front widows.

She even made a bread-and-butter pudding and sent it to Anita's maid, hoping they will have it for evening tea. Rose was walking in and out of her apartment, anticipating some sign of their activities.

As a last resort, she made a Creamy Pumpkin Soup with bay leaves and then took it herself around five thirty p.m. and gave it to Tharanga the maid. She knew her prayers would be answered soon. So, they were! Exactly at 5.42 p.m., one curtain opened and Anita waved to her, though she was pretending that she was attending to her flower plot. She could see the silhouette of a tall person behind Anita, when she said: "Darling, I sent you some soup, try it, it's good for a hang-over"

"OK, Aunty Rose, thank you, very kind of you, we are famished!" Rose was ecstatic. She happily and contentedly retired into her abode.

CHAPTER 10

Ranga entered the incident room of the Central Province DIG's office. Every officer stood up and saluted him. Having acknowledged the salutes, Ranga saluted the DIG of the Central Province.

"Officer, please take a front seat"

DIG Silva who was conducting the meeting, shook hands with Ranga.

After the introductions were made, SI Pathirana who was the IT specialist, started his power- point presentation of the Crime Report. It was very well done, condensing every little detail into an abstract form where one could study the case without going through bulky reports. Ranga was very impressed and he felt that was an excellent start.

However, the old school DIG, preferred a traditional and time-tested 'Crime Fact Board,' – where you either write or pin various pieces of information on a board, as more and more facts are gathered by the team.

As per the DIG's advice, a board was set up in the conference room. It had the advantage of displaying all the important points in one place and being visible all the time. More and more notes or pictures could be added to it as new evidence surfaced.

Just by looking at it, one could solve even the most mysterious and complicated cases. It could pool the ideas in an open forum for everyone to see, without having to attend meetings.

At the end of the briefing, Ranga asked SI Pathirana to email the presentation to him.

After the meeting, Ranga was shown to his temporary quarters in the Police Barracks, Officers' section. It was just a minimally furnished room and as soon as he entered, he felt very lonely and miserable. He neither had anyone to speak to nor anyone known to him.

Around six thirty p.m., he walked up to the officers' mess, which was empty.

The lone bartender was in a pensive mood, listening to Adagio for Strings in B-Flat Minor by Orchestra da Camera Fiorentina and Giuseppe Lanzetta.

Ranga felt like throttling the miserable soul, but decided otherwise. The bartender was a Police Constable and Ranga was surprised as to why he was listening to such highbrow classical music.

"What can I get you, sir?" He saluted Ranga. "Don't you have better music?"

"Drink?"

"Do you have Elvis Presley, anything? and I would like a beer"

"Coming up Sir!" The bartender kicked out of his melancholic mood, poured a beer with a thick head of froth and went near the ancient gramophone which reminded him of Anita's 'grumpy,' He took out the equally old cardboard box behind it and selected an LP.

"Presley it is." It started with a crackling sound and then Presley wanted to wear his Blue Suede Shoes, followed by a bit of Jail House Rock.

However, Ranga promised himself this murderer was not going to rock inside the jail or even rot inside it. Anyway, he was going to make sure it was gallows and nothing but gallows, for him.

The beer and the music perked up his and the bartender's moods, but there was something missing to complete the famous saying.

"Wine, Women and Song!" Anita!

He just stared at the beer which was disappearing at a rate and he imagined Anita looking at him. He suddenly remembered that he had forgotten to ring her at all. He knew he was going to get an earful, and he was right!

"You have forgotten me already? What is that music? Are there any WPC's around?" The questioning went on ad nauseam!

For the first time in his life, he got a taste of what to expect in a relationship!

He just listened and listened. He knew there was no point apologizing. When she eventually finished her outburst, "I am feeling very lonely here and I miss you a lot," he was a quick learner. He was surprised when she asked in a subdued tone,

"Do you really miss me?"

"Yes, darling," he ordered another beer and he badly needed one! "Ranga, are you working over the weekend as well?"

"Not really, unless there's any new development."

"I have to go and visit my mother over the weekend and she wants me to introduce you to her," "Are you sure?"

"Yes she is impatient to meet you. On Friday, on my way there, I'll pick you up and on Monday morning, I can drop you back there."

"That sounds exciting."

He was elated and gulped the rest of the beer in one go! Elvis was playing havoc and Ranga noticed that a few officers had trickled in and were enjoying the maestro. He decided to call it a day.

On Friday, around six thirty p.m., he saw the mighty 'red beast,' turning into the Officers' quarters. As a matter of fact, he had been ready since four p.m. He had already packed his sports shoulder bag and his personal weapon in its holster was lying at the bottom of the bag. From the first floor, he waved to her, so she would know that he was ready.

This was the very first time Ranga had got into a Continental car. The full grain genuine leather seats, high-mounted dash board with walnut fascia, 'two-spoke,' steering wheel and original Jaguar radio in its pristine condition, was a novelty to this officer who had been driven around in diesel jeeps, all these years. Even his private vehicle was a Toyota hatchback, which had seen better days. His fairly meager income, sans the usual cut-backs others indulged in, did not allow him the luxury of a more modern vehicle.

No doubt the red beast would have been the cynosure of all eyes at the barracks!

The seat was so comfortable, and he was just gazing around at the interior, when he noticed that Anita was wearing a short pair of shorts, exposing her shapely and smooth thighs right up to the top.

"Mister, where are you looking, don't you think a hello and a kiss would be more appropriate?" Ranga felt ashamed and turned toward Anita and kissed her left cheek.

"Do you always look at women's legs first?" He didn't have anything to say.

However, his desire to rip her clothes off and make love to her right then and there, was the only thing that crossed his mind.

"I know what you are thinking!" No comment forthcoming.

Ranga was surprised. He could feel the power of the engine and the comfort it gives the passengers. Anita's reflexes were so brisk and on that day, he realized the meaning of 'man and machine in harmony,' something he had never experienced before.

She was concentrating on her driving, so Ranga had all the time to enjoy the beauty of an exceptional woman whom he thought he was falling in love with. He began drifting off to his own fairy-tale world.

She was on top of a mountain, wearing a long white see-through dress against the setting Sun. Rabbits were frolicking, and she was trying to touch them. Against the setting orange-red sunrays, he could see her body contour through her dress. The more he tried to touch her; the more he got close to her, the more she drifted away from him.

Suddenly, he was rudely interrupted, "oi, I am driving here, talk to me!"

The drive was only 30 kilometers as the crow flew. However, it took more than one hour to reach their destination, due to narrow winding roads with steep slopes. The headlights of the Jaguar were not that powerful, due to this model being able to accommodate only normal bulbs.

When the car pulled over near the car-port, Ranga saw Anita's mother waiting near the front door, leaning against the 'Halmilla,' door frame, gazing out anxiously.

Anita hopped off the car and virtually ran toward her mother, kneeled before her and worshipped her as per the SriLankan custom. Ranga, hailing from the coastal town of Moratuwa and being a Christian, was not too familiar with such a custom, though he had to get acquainted with it in the line of duty, when he had to visit temples. He also followed Anita.

With tearful eyes, Helen blessed him, 'the probable future husband of Anita.' Then Helen kissed him on both cheeks, cupping his jaw with both her hands.

This macho man couldn't hold back his tears which were wiped away by Helen from the corner of the 'Ossari,' she was wearing and Anita saw it. This made Anita also to break down in tears. This was the very first time in his life, Ranga had worshipped a human being in that sense.

One could say that moment was the 'Mother of all emotions!' where they were concerned, a term that entered the vocabulary in recent years, presumably after the Iraq war. The moment was so intense that all three of them hugged one another spontaneously, creating an enduring bond which even surpassed super-glue by far. No one wanted to let the moment go, until Anita spoke, "*Ammi*, this is Ranga, Ranga this is my mother Helen," That reminded Ranga of the famous last words of Jesus Christ whilst he was crucified and dying.

By the same token, he realized Jesus Christ died on the cross and wondered "is this my cross?" Yet again, Ranga had chosen this on his own free will and was quite happy about it. He was overwhelmed with emotions and this time he couldn't avoid crying.

Descending from an 'ordinary family,' from Moratuwa, he was mesmerized by the class and refinement of this household. A sense of insecurity and apprehension took over his thought process, whether he could cope or if this was an illusion, somewhat like a mirage?

A spotlessly maintained, artistic, cracked white marble floor which reminded him of the old films of the Roman era; the airy, spacious veranda, furnished with Ebony planter's reclining chairs called 'Hansi Putuwa,' a massive Jak wood 'Dutch Box,' referred to locally as a 'Pettagama,' and above all, a huge English Grandfather clock, looking at him with suspicious eyes, made him feel somewhat uneasy.

While he was just looking at this intimidating face of the clock, it chimed nine times, making his heart stop momentarily. Was it a warning? Not only once but nine times!

"You children, I have prepared the guest room. Anita why not show him the way?"

After dinner, Helen retired to her room and Anita decided to stay with Ranga in the guest room. "Ranga, tell me about the progress of your inquiry."

Ranga got a USB and gave it to Anita. It contained a power-point presentation and various other information.

"So, let's summarize this. No actual eyewitnesses. The only witness was a little boy who frequented that spot where they found the body, with this girl many times. Apparently both of them had gone to the stream around nine a.m. and sat on the boulder and were chatting away for about half an hour. Then this boy's mother called him and the girl just stayed back.

When he was climbing the steep and slippery access foot path, he heard the sound of a bird call which both of them had heard before on numerous occasions. They had never really seen any bird though. The boy remembered that sound, because when they were there on previous occasions as well, they had heard it and had tried to locate it by crossing the stream a few times, since it appeared to come from the jungle side, but without any success.

"That side is the nature reserve with plenty of birds," Ranga tried to place it down as non-relevant. However, Anita was not convinced.

She looked at Ranga, the look which said it all! The universally accepted expression of a woman without uttering a word! Ranga had a lot to learn. I don't agree with you. For the first time in his life, he learnt a new thing, 'the unwritten law of female communication,' – The look! – 'I don't agree or don't do it!'

"Yes, you got a point there worth considering," damage control achieved instantly. "Ranga you must speak to this kid and visit the site with him."

Was it the trance he was in or the valuable suggestion Anita made? One cannot say if Ranga decided to act upon it in that instant or whether he had it in the back of his mind already. He rang the SI who had made the presentation. "Can you arrange to visit the site tomorrow? and I need to speak to that little boy."

Ranga saw a smile on her face.

The following morning at the breakfast table;

"Anita, the Police jeep is coming at nine a.m. to take me there, would you like to join me?"

No, darling it's not appropriate, I'll drive there myself, I would like to study the case for my research."

"In that case, can you take me there? I can ask the police team to go there straight." "That sounds good, is it okay for you to go there separately?"

"Of course, it is, the defense lawyer is not going to ask me one day, how I arrived at the crime scene."

Overjoyed, Anita with a flirty salute, "OK Officer, I shall deliver you to the crime scene, unless the officer himself decides to embark upon any inappropriate activity during his duty."

As a matter of fact, making love to her on the back seat of the Jaguar, had crossed his mind that very moment.

"OK madam, I accept your offer, though I cannot promise that inappropriate action would not ensue." He grabbed her hand and squeezed it tightly. Anita felt her whole body warming up, and she wished he would make love to her on the breakfast table itself, leaving aside a back seat romance. She seemed to have subconsciously read his mind.

"We can leave at eight a.m. and I have asked them to go there at nine a.m."

Both of them got up and walked toward the room. On their way to the room, Ranga noticed the Grandfather's clock, the bully, looking at him with a straight flat face, with two unequal sticks, the longer one pointing straight down and the shorty pointing in between Roman numbers seven and eight with the solitary pendulum swaying away in an orderly fashion.

He didn't like the clock face and he went near it,

'Look here mate, one of these days I am going to make love to her in front of you, you big bully.' Noticing Ranga's face very close to the dial, "Darling what's up?"

"No, I promised something to this Grandfather." Anita just shook her head and entered the room.

On their way to the crime scene, which was a good one hour's drive that goes through the nature reserve; all of a sudden, Anita stopped the car in front of a small tea boutique by the roadside.

When Ranga inquired "What do you want?" without talking to him, Anita got down and walked toward the tea boutique. He saw her pointing to the big wide mouthed plastic bottle which contained sweets and she bought all the sweets in it.

The estate road leading to the laborers' quarters commonly known as 'line rooms,' was a narrow gravel road with patches of asphalt here and there, indicating that probably for a few decades, it has been thoroughly neglected.

The Jaguar didn't like the road, yet it obeyed its mistress.

A Police jeep was parked in front of the terraced houses, and a sizable number of estate workers had gathered around.

Anita pulled up the Jaguar next to the Police Jeep. There were four Police personnel, of which one was a WPC.

When Ranga and Anita got down from the flashy red Jaguar from both sides simultaneously, it was like a typical 'cinema set,' of a Bollywood film. Anita, who was wearing tight blue Levi's jeans, a cream-colored kind of see-through blouse which distinctly showed the black bra she was wearing, and tapering dark blue sunglasses; was the cynosure of all eyes!

Here enters the heroine and the hero of the film. The Police officers saluted their superior and he introduced the professor to them.

Though the WPC was not amused, all the male police officers were mesmerized by the professor and were trying to get a chance to talk to her.

The SI led them to the house of the victim, which was situated at the middle of the line. Ranga had to virtually bend in half to enter the one roomed house, since the front door frame was only five feet in height. Anita opted out of going into the house. There were about ten to fifteen children of various ages, some with broad smiles and talkative, others with frozen faces of fear or apprehension.

Anita's attention was directed toward a small boy of around four years of age, who appeared to be very disturbed and isolated.

"What's your name?" He did not answer. Watching this, the WPC came near her, "Madam, he doesn't speak the language."

Then only did Anita realize it. The WPC was fluent in Tamil.

"Madam, he is the last one to see the victim at the stream." Anita took out the sweets she had brought. Within no time, about twenty children surrounded her. She distributed the sweets amongst all of them. They started smiling and became very talkative.

From a distance, Ranga realized his presence made them scared. So, he called the WPC and instructed her that whilst he and the others interviewed the adults, both Anita and the WPC were to talk to the children.

Every child took a liking to Anita, and she asked the WPC to ask who had seen the victim, Gowri, that day. A little boy said he was with her around nine a.m. that day, sitting at their favorite spot on a flat boulder and throwing pebbles into the stream. The WPC was very good with her communication and she built up a good rapport with the child. Anita suggested to the little boy to take them to the spot. All three of them climbed down to the stream and sat on the exact spot he had described. Translated by the WPC, Anita asked a few questions,

"Murugan do you come here with Gowri often?"

"Yes," "Are the others also coming here?

"Yes"

"Do you come alone?"

"Sometimes, but Gowri comes here alone often." "That day were you with her?"

"Yes but she asked me to go back to my house and she stayed behind."

Anita's sweets had an unbelievable response from all the children who opened up to both Anita and the WPC. Every bit of information was written down with all the details, by the WPC.

The whole team came down to inspect the site. Armed with the boy's information, Anita knew it was worth inspecting the other side of the stream.

"Officer, I think we should inspect the other side of the stream," Anita said in a rather official way.

"Yes, Professor."

SSP Ranga instructed his subordinates to prepare for it. The team which included a photographer, went back to the jeep and brought gum boots, gloves and crime-scene luminous jackets with them. Whilst they were preparing themselves, agile Anita had just jumped from boulder to boulder like a frog and reached the other side within no time.

However, the rather heavy-weight WPC couldn't even clear the very first boulder. Due to fear and inability, she decided to stay back and keep writing the notes which she was good at.

The team, with heavy gum boots, found it very difficult to walk about as well, especially over the boulders. Ranga was no better in that respect, in comparison to his professional team. Seeing that Anita had gone to the other side already, "Professor, be careful, please wait for us" Whether she heard or not, she just disappeared behind another boulder.

Ranga was concerned and asked his SI to speed up and follow her quickly. However, even the young and fit SI was not much better with his gum boots and he was also struggling to walk.

According to Murugan, they had heard an unusual bird sound on many occasions, and Little Gowri had been very secretive about something. She had given some very tasty sweets he had never even seen before and asked him to keep it only to himself.

After swearing that he will never divulge that she had given these sweets to him and promising not to give it to anyone else; she had herself put these sweets into his mouth, after asking him to close his eyes. Further to that, he has noticed Gowri had some expensive color pencils which she hid from everybody, and he was told she was going to kill him if he was going to tell anyone.

Then she had spat on her palm and asked him to do so as well and squeezed his hands.

Only once, when he saw Gowri secretly going toward the stream, he had followed her and before reaching the stream, he had seen a silhouette of a figure wearing something like a soldier's jungle color sarong and similar shirt, but disappeared never to be seen again.

Anita inspected the area that Murugan had described. There was nothing unusual, except for some animal footprints which she could not identify.

Then she heard, "Professor wait up!" The jungle side looked scary, so Anita sat on a small boulder nearby.

Then she heard the distant voices of the team getting closer, a splash, "be careful," and an "I am okay". A few minutes later, the SI appeared first, fully drenched, carrying his gum boots in his hands.

"Madam, how did you manage?"

With a surprised and at the same time, beaten and shameful look, seeing Anita sitting like a queen on a throne, on the rock, in pristine condition. The SI was panting heavily. He was followed by the rest of the team, looking no better than the SI.

When Ranga saw Anita, he was amazed and had an impulse to hug her and kiss her passionately. However, Anita was in a more serious mood.

"Officer, we have to search the surrounding area well. At the preliminary inspection, they have covered the other side of the stream thoroughly, but not this side."

Ranga instructed the team to comply. On that side of the stream, the bank was not that steep in comparison to this side. On this side, thick vegetation, small and large boulders and huge conifer trees were abundant. The SI took the lead walking barefoot, followed by Ranga and his team. Anita, dropped back and kept following them, whilst inspecting the surroundings carefully herself. Nothing of significance was seen.

Then they noticed that there appeared to be a kind of a track extending into the interior. The SI started walking through it, followed by the rest.

A good 200 meters interior, it led to a cleared area, close to a huge rock face. At the foot of the rock, was an open cave with plenty of space at the entrance but which narrowed to a height about 2 to 3 feet toward the end.

Outside, there was an area with a thick growth of wild grass and some patches of gravel. There appeared to be numerous animal footprints and a strange area with a high concentration of various other footprints without any set pattern. Then they noticed some animal droppings which appeared to be of big animals such as cattle or buffalo.

Ranga was baffled by this, because wild animals did not need to hang around in the area, as there was nothing of use to a wild animal there.

While the police team were inspecting the area, Anita sat on the flat rock at the base of the rock face, near the entrance to the cave.

She was in deep thought about this murder and something told her the murderer would have been here.
On the surface of the rock base, there were numerous little crevices ranging from a few inches to a foot. As a matter of fact, she was sitting, covering a small crevice about 3 inches deep. One hour later, Ranga decided to terminate the inspection.

"Professor, we have finished, we didn't find anything except an end of a shoelace about 2 inches long. These animal footprints are weird. They have photographed everything. Let's go"

Anita got up from where she was seated and as she took the

first step, she notice something stuck in the crevice. She bent over and with the greatest difficulty, picked it up.

It was a crumpled part of a toffee wrapper.

She called the SI and he took it with a pair of forceps, placed it in a plastic specimen bag and asked the photographer to photograph the site.

They headed back to their vehicles. As soon as they reached the vehicles, about fifteen children came and surrounded Anita's Jaguar, admiring the vehicle and anticipating more sweets.

"Professor, follow us, we are going to the incident room at the DIG's office." And Ranga got into the front seat of the Police Jeep. As she was about to close the door, she noticed Murugan was standing almost touching the door. Anita got out of the car and called out to the SI who was about to board the Jeep. The older villagers had been warned to stay clear of the area in case they interfered with any clues that may be of use to the investigators.

"Can you bring me that sweet wrapper, please?" Anita requested.

She asked Murugan to follow her toward the jeep, got the specimen bag and showed the sweet wrapper to him. Watching this, the WPC got down from the jeep,

"Professor what do you want to ask?"

"Can you ask him whether he can recognize this and whether Gowri gave him sweets with this type of wrappers?"

Murugan looked at it carefully and said it was the same color, but was not too sure. Anita thanked the little boy and got into the car.

The DIG's office incident room was almost full. Police officers, forensics, lab personnel.

Anita looked a bit out of place and she just sat right at

the back, unnoticed. Ranga was presiding over the proceedings. She didn't quite understand the conversations and the presentations that were going on.

She was almost about to go into a deep sleep when she heard the SI mentioning "Here I have a list of possible pieces of evidence we found at the crime scene."

She instantly became alert and got up from her semi-slumber and was listening to the items collected at the crime scene. The SI laid out everything found so far at the crime scene, including those found that morning, on the table. There wasn't anything of significance worth inquiring about, everyone thought.

Once proceedings were over, all the other participants left. Ranga was collecting a few of the documents given to him. Then he noticed Anita coming forward.

"Oh, sorry I ignored you. OK, we can go back now."

"Yeah, I suppose." Nevertheless, Ranga noticed there was something worrying Anita.

"Are you OK, Anita? You seem to be distant."

"No, I am OK, let's go home."

Both got into the car and drove off. Within a few minutes, Anita jammed on the brake as if they were about to run over a man. The car skidded to a jarring halt and if it were not for the seat belt Ranga was wearing, plastic surgeons would have had to pay a substantial amount of tax!

"Women drivers," was Ranga's spontaneous response.

Anita made a three point turn so fast; Ranga's head started spinning like a merry-go-round. "What?" annoyed, Ranga barked.

She started driving like a maniac. "What's wrong with you

Anita?"

Ranga shouted at the top of his voice. She didn't say anything at all, until the car came to the DIG's office premises. The car came to a screeching halt with a cloud of dust, just missing the flag pole in front of the office by an inch!

"What the hell? Talk to me, Professor!" annoyed, Ranga got down from the car, bewildered as to what was happening to Anita.

"Officer, I need to see all the artifacts recovered from the crime scene on the first day," Anita said in an equally official and challenging tone.

The sentry guarding the gates was at a loss for words, to see a woman giving orders to an SSP. Though he wanted to know what it was about, his better sense advised him against it.

'A sprat like me better not reach turbulent waters when sharks and whales play,' and looked at the road as if nothing had happened.

Ranga and Anita came to the incident room which was deserted. Ranga ordered his SI to bring all the artifacts recovered. Anita asked the SI to empty all the items collected from the first day, onto the desk. She put on a pair of gloves and started rummaging through little plastic pieces, bottle tops, various paper pieces, soft drink cans, aluminum and metal pieces; but she picked up only a small piece of toffee wrapper.

By this time, there were a few officers watching this scene and an experienced Crime Prevention Officer, whispered in his colleague's ear "Nutty Professor," which Ranga heard but pretended not to hear, since he was experiencing a similar trend of thought.

Anita was looking at the partial toffee wrapper, turning it around quite a few times and asked for a clear picture of this to be forwarded to her.

Big men, the elite of crime prevention squad's minds were synchronized in unison, 'Psychologists are mad – Beyond any doubt', as they would even prove in front of a judge.

Ranga was no exception.

Every officer present thought, 'this evening the officer's mess 'specialty,' would be 'The Nutty Professor and Her Slave Officer,'

Anita thanked everyone profusely and apologized for her intrusion. Ranga just remained a passive observer.

CHAPTER 11

Anita looked out of her window to see her only relative in Colombo, kneeling before her rose bush and pruning it with much love and affection. Fifty-nine years of age, still a spinster, her Aunt Rose was somewhat of a mysterious character she thought. A lively, smart and jovial person, how could she end up as a spinster? This was the million-dollar question Anita had been trying to find the answer for many years!

A sense of fear, desperation and hopelessness engulfed her like a humongous black cloud, that one day, she may end up like her dear aunt. Being a psychologist, she thought she must practice what she preached; so, the answer was to confront the issue direct and that was what she decided to do next.

"Aunty Rose, would you like to have lunch with me?" It was a Sunday. Rose put the secateurs away and looked up at the window to see Anita waiting anxiously for an answer.

"All right dear, I'll bring the wine, I have got a vintage red waiting to be opened for the last three years, I suppose the time is ripe to savor it."

Anita felt that cloudy screen between her and Aunt Rose could be wiped out forever, if she could get her Aunt to open up her heart to her.

When she arrived, Rose was wearing a Maria Kaftan by Chic Le Frique, which Anita had never seen her wearing before. Keeping to her promise, she carried with her a bottle of vintage Chateau Neuf-de-Pape red, to match her dress, in that sense of class and refinement.

The fifty-nine-year-old Rose, showed her colors of 'wine etiquette,' by opening the vintage bottle with the traditional corkscrew she had with her and leaving it open for the wine, trapped in the bottle waiting like a genie all these years; to breathe its share of air to bring out the best of its taste and refinement!

Anita was so impressed when her Aunt Rose pulled out the cork, by first slowly twisting the corkscrew very gently all the way in and while gripping the bottle between her shapely thighs, pulling it out in one go, with a pleasing 'pop,' sound.

What a maestro! she thought.

Anita was impatient to taste the wine.

However, Rose was not in a hurry. She asked Anita to go and sit on the Christopher Knight Home Tafton, Tufted Leather Club chair, in the lounge area. Whilst the wine was breathing its air, Rose opened the ebony wine glass cabinet and took out two Italian hand-crafted Arte di Murano, tall Red Glass Goblets which Anita had never seen previously, though it was her father's wine glass cabinet. Tharanga the maid, washed the wine glasses very carefully, as this was the first time she too had seen such unusual glasses to drink wine in.

Once the wine was poured in gently but steadily, both sat facing each other with the goblets in their hands and assumed comfortable postures as they relaxed.

With the warmth of the wine permeating through her, Aunt Rose began to open up.

"Yes dear, you are my only relative. I was thinking all these years that I must have this little talk with you, especially as your father is no more, and you ought to know this."

Anita started sipping the wine slowly but Rose was much quicker with her first glass.

"As you are well aware, I do not own any real estate and all this is your father's which I am enjoying. I don't have anything," while topping her glass up.

With that statement, Anita wondered how come she led a rich person's life all these years. It was Rose's time, so Anita thought,

'I'll just listen, and I'm not going to ask any questions, unless of course, she invites me to ask questions.'

"Your father was very good to me, he looked after me all these years, I am ten years younger to him, and he loved me very much. I don't know why my parents decided to educate me in Colombo, instead of Kandy, where good schools were available even then and I would have traveled from home to school.

But for some strange reason, they decided to send me to Colombo; and that was the time they bought this property from a British tea broker. I was left in the hands of a very capable and trustworthy nanny who looked after me devotedly. I was taken home to Kandy only once a month.

Every now and then, my mother came to Colombo and stayed with me. I was very confused about that, because even when I went home, I felt they did not want me to associate with the house staff. I remember sometimes, when the kitchen staff tried to come and speak to me, they were chased away by my mother.

She was very protective of me, and she made sure she was with me all the time when I was at home. Later, when your dad came from UK, he established his Colombo chambers here. So, I moved to the 'front stables,' house which it was called then, where as you know, I live now. I had a very strange childhood living in Colombo, when my parents were living mainly in Kandy."

Rose poured another glass for herself, then got up and kept

the glass on a table, "I'll be back in a minute."

She virtually ran to her abode and came back within no time, with a tightly packed tin with various nuts she had bought in Indonesia.

Aunt Rose started pouring her heart out.

"When I was small, I was occupying this house and I was looked after by this nanny for many years. You must be itching to know why I'm not married. When I was in my twenties, I worked in our father's friend's tea brokerage company. I had a few lovers but they were not husband material.

Later, I met your father's junior lawyer who was very handsome and I was very hopeful and was madly in love. Tragically, he committed suicide. I simply don't know why. That was the end of my love life and since then, have never met anyone worth considering.

So, here I am, your Aunty Rose, having a drink with you just by myself." Anita emptied her glass and helped herself to a refill. After munching on some pistachios and walnuts, she wanted to ask her aunt about how she survived all these years and her source of income; Then again, she thought the time was probably not right and decided to wait until she opened up some more.

Rose finished her third glass and was looking at it blankly; without even looking at Anita.

"You must be wandering from where I get my money." and looked at Anita eye to eye. My father had another huge estate on the other side of the nature reserve, which he inherited from my mother's side and had given to one of his friends to manage; and the deal was for him to pay me half of the income. He is a very honest and honorable person. Up to date, he sends me my share."

With raised eyebrows, Anita said "My father never ever

mentioned such a thing to me," in a somewhat resentful tone.

Rose tried to play it down.

However, Anita's mind was working. Eventually, she had to be the heir to that property as well.

Anita felt Rose was getting uncomfortable and being a psychologist, she felt her aunt was regretting divulging this information to her. She decided not to ask about it unless Aunty Rose volunteered the information.

"You know darling I was also in the dark as to why I was kept in Colombo without any reason at all, so your father not telling you, doesn't surprise me. It appears '*Wickramasooriyas*,' have many skeletons in the cupboard!"

Anita just entered the land of the unknown and the sad part was, it was her own land. She was quite disturbed about what she heard.

However, she tried to put up a brave face. She was a maestro in bottling up emotions, yet something like this family secret, she was not able to absorb easily. Rose saw Anita's changing mood and decided to bail her out of this. It would have been the best option for both of them, yet she was reluctant to let go of this finest wine.

"OK dear let's finish this and eat."

Anita also realized there was no point getting upset over these intriguing events. Anyway, she had inherited massive wealth already. She also had a lucrative practice as a renowned Psychologist.

"Let's eat then, Tharanga, can you lay the table please," and she got up and shared the rest of the wine equally between the two of them.

Whilst eating, neither of them spoke much. The quality wine was making them both feel mellow.

Anita's mind was torturing her to know more about this phantom friend Aunt Rose had mentioned.

Her assumption was that the friend probably was her aunt's lover, and she promised herself she was going to dig into the bottom of this eventually.

After the sumptuous lunch, Rose retired to her abode having exchanged a few affectionate hugs.

However, Anita was very restless not learning anything of value; and the statement her aunt made "Wickramasooriyas have many skeletons in the cupboard," started torturing her so much that even Satan may have looked like a softie. Her mind was an exploding inferno, like a nuclear reactor!

'I am going to start this crusade now, even if I have to turn the 'Ayers Rock,' upside down! As they say, 'Everything must start from home,' Anita thought, 'I am going to start here and start now! She was kind of 'tipsy,' a few moments ago, due to the vintage Chateau.

Instant transformation! She felt sort of fully sober and energetic the very next moment.

As soon as Tharanga saw her mistress wearing her corduroy shorts and oversized faded sweatshirt; and especially when madam folded the sleeves up, she knew she'll be making gallons of coffee tonight!

Tharanga checked whether they had enough biscuits to last the night. Tharanga also changed to denim pants and a T-shirt herself.

It was only after three months after her father's passing away; nothing has been touched and her father's room was still locked.

"Tharanga where is the key?"

"Wait madam, I'll check in the key box"

She brought a bunch of keys in an ancient, rather huge, copper alloy ring. There were ten keys altogether. While just one key was attached to a separate ring, the rest were on the main ring. She tried to open the door with those keys and succeeded with the fourth one she tried.

The 'Sooriyamara,' door opened reluctantly with a loud creak. The room was pitch dark and with the light from the mobile phone, Anita managed to find the light switch. The room smelled moldy and was very warm and stuffy inside.

In spite of it, she felt the old spice and tobacco aromas, which brought tears to her eyes. "Tharanga, can you open the curtains and the windows please?"

As soon as Tharanga opened them, the angled sunrays started streaming in and the whole room came alive. The 'four-poster' king sized bed, the 'Nadun,' almirah with intricate carvings, the pure ebony dressing table with a traditional ancient oval 'tiltable mirror,' with carvings matching those on the almirah, the five-drawer chest of drawers, an easy chair and a small clothes rack, all started talking to Anita, simultaneously.

While she listened to them, Tharanga noticed her mistress was crying. Tharanga did not want to disturb the conversation, "Madam, I'll be in the kitchen if you need me."

The 'conversation,' was so intense that Anita didn't even notice her. She sat on the bed and lay down. The mosquito net hung above, was crying too!

Her memories about her father started flowing out like an open sluice gate, and she intentionally jumped into the gushing flow to drown in it.

Once the flow subsided, she felt that she was floating, only to realize that she had actually fallen asleep!

The time was five thirty in the evening.

The setting sun was making a desperate attempt to deliver

its ever-angulating, now feeble rays, to help Anita reminisce her past.

She realized that she was still holding on to the key ring. After wiping away her tears with her baggy sweatshirt sleeve which was drenched in sweat, while she was asleep, she got up and went near the almirah.

At the second attempt, the almirah opened. Ignoring all the clothes, she opened the twin-level narrow drawers. Every almirah had a secret drawer which was pretty standard, and the opening mechanisms were also somewhat standard. Since she knew how to open other almirahs at home, this wasn't a problem.

She did not want Tharanga to see anything she was doing. So, she closed the door and emptied the drawers onto the bed. Apart from common things you would expect in drawers like this, there was nothing of any significance. Then she checked all the other drawers in the dressing table and the five-drawer chest of drawers.

She opened the door.

"Tharanga, can you bring those extra-large garbage bags? I want to send all Appachchi's (father's) clothes to the dry cleaners."

Tharanga brought the full packet which contained twelve garbage bags. "Thank you." And she was about to close the door again.

"Madam, can I make a coffee?"

"That would be nice, thanks."

She left the door ajar. Anita started emptying the almirah first, after checking every pocket of all the garments carefully. Apart from a substantial amount of money, various receipts which she checked and found inconsequential, and quite a few pens, there was nothing of real substance.

One black jacket contained a fungus covered wedding cake and in another one she found his wedding ring which she very carefully kept separately.

She put all the garments which were checked, into the garbage bags. While sipping the coffee, Anita managed to clear everything within two hours. There were seven bags full of garments. She just sat on the bed and asked Tharanga to put all the bags into the jeep.

Only then did she notice that one key was smaller and different from the others and had its own separate ring. She guessed it probably belonged to a small box or something.

However, she did not find anything to open with that key. There were two more keys which were not of use while one was rather humongous and had carvings on it. Anita guessed it was the key to the 'Dutch Box,' in the veranda. When she came to the lounge area, she realized the remaining key would be for the wine glass cabinet; and it was.

She went to the Dutch Box and inserted the big key and it opened. She lifted the heavy lid with the greatest difficulty. It was full of house plans and antique books; and she was pleasantly surprised when she saw an original copy of 'The Natural History of Ceylon,' by Emmerson Tennent, in pristine condition, yet covered with a thick layer of dust.

She knew it was a collector's item and could fetch millions, though she would never sell it!

She started sneezing heavily and her runny nose turned into a 'downpour.' She closed the box and locked it again, sans the 'Tennent.' She continued to sneeze.

"Tharanga, please bring my hair drier."

With the hair drier, she expelled the dust particles as much as possible, after carefully opening all the pages. Then she wet a micro fiber duster and wiped the outer cover gently with it, making sure it wouldn't harm the book. After switching on the ceiling fan, she kept the book on a little stool under the fan and left it to dry.

As soon as she went into her room, she removed all her clothes, put them into the dirty linen basket and kept it outside the door still naked. She went straight to the shower and opened it fully.

The dust washed away in no time and the second line of attack, the Skin Solace body scrub, did not have any mercy on the hidden dust particles.

It was like washing away one's sins with prayers!

She stepped out of the shower feeling rejuvenated and energetic, though she continued sneezing occasionally.

Her hair was wet, so she wrapped it with the face towel, intermingling her hair like a turban.

Still naked, she came out of the bathroom and walked across the room toward her wardrobe, passing her much-loved mirror.

Her eyes always helped her to reassure herself of her beauty, shapely body and above all, her 'sky worshipping,' nipples from the reflections off the mirror.

Though she reassured herself thus, she noticed her red-shot sclera and a mild swelling of the eyelids.

"Bloody hell, I am allergic to dust! Hope it's not bloody Tennent who imposed unfair direct taxes on poor Ceylonese people to compensate for losses made due to reducing cinnamon and coffee export tax from Ceylon; just because UK was in an economic depression in 1845."

Her anti-colonial sentiment sprang up like a mushroom.

However, she followed and enjoyed all the Colonial Masters,' habits and life styles inculcated on the elite of Ceylon, whilst at the same time, criticizing it.

She got panicky when she saw the swollen eyelids. "Tharanga, where is my piriton?" still looking at her eyes at close range, she shouted. Hearing the commotion, Tharanga came running into the room, to see her mistress fully naked except for a weird turban.

"OK, madam I'll bring, it is in the medicine cabinet in the kitchen" and ran even without closing the door.

On her way to the kitchen, she just looked at her own wobbly body, and was not even able to see her feet without bending over, while her wobbling bosom heaved like a break dancer.

She promised herself that she would reduce her rice intake, stop eating all the expensive chocolates her mistress brought and use the exercise machine more often when her mistress went to work.

After taking a couple of piriton tablets, she put on the Paddington Bear night shirt gifted to her by her father and hit the sack, reminiscing her childhood days.

CHAPTER 12

Michael read the Sunday Times with much enthusiasm after seeing the headlines,

'Murder by the Stream,'

The account of a mysterious death of a young girl of seven years in his neighborhood, made him proud and a sense of superiority engulfed his starved, mindset which was harboring an inferiority complex.

He was glad; he had achieved the much-desired crest of the wave in eliminating the weak and the useless, but he realized he had a long way to go to reach the very pinnacle in showing the world that he was no longer a mental weakling!

He felt that his years of meticulous planning had paid off. He had a sarcastic smile on his face when he realized that the police were clueless about it and even unsure whether it was an accident or a murder.

He read it for the second time and he couldn't help himself laughing out loudly; how stupid the police were!

From a distance, 'Appu,' the butler saw his master laughing to himself and decided not to disturb him.

He was about to turn back,

"Appu, can you tell Banda to wash my MG?"

Nicolaus was surprised, how come master saw him, because master was looking the other way and was drowned in his own deep thoughts and laughter.

"Yes Sir,"

Michael went inside his room and stopped near the huge one-inch scale map of the forest reserve, which he had got from the Surveyor General himself.

Since his estate was bordering one of the perimeters of the nature reserve, his estate was also clearly shown on the map. The nature reserve was situated in the valley in-between a group of mountains surrounding it. It was 15 kilometers by 10 kilometers, stretch. At the perimeter, along one side, a winding major 'A' road was situated.

Even though 'as the crow flies,' it was only about 15 kilometers, the winding road became a good 40 km long stretch.

Right in the middle, there was a stream bisecting the reserve into two portions. Since it was situated at the lowest point of the valley, the stream, with numerous boulders and rocks, was more or less like a river; in comparison to the small tributaries that drained into it.

He was studying the map thoroughly with an intent of sorts.

His attention was directed toward the little village which was right opposite, bordering the river at the far end, away from his estate.

One could see his pupils becoming dilated with excitement as he made his decision.

The telephone at the 'Sembu Rest,' started ringing. Its owner Piyal, picked up the phone himself, to hear Michael Hamu's voice with a distinctly posh accent, at the other end.

He was extremely pleased to hear Michael Hamu's voice, since Hamu had helped him to buy this property overlooking the river at a higher elevation; to establish the family run restaurant and 'bed and breakfast.' He was eternally indebted to him!

"Yes Sir, it is so nice to hear your voice, what can I do for you, Hamu?"

"Piyal, I want to come and have lunch with you, I am sorry I was not able to visit you for the last three years."

"Oh Hamu, it's an honor and a privilege to have you here, how many are coming?" "It's only me."

As soon as Piyal kept the phone,

"Menike, Michael Hamu is coming to have lunch with us, I'll bring something to cook."

He got into his three-wheeler which was parked in front of his restaurant and went toward town.

Michael did not waste any time. He had a 40 km drive. He took his Nikon Aculon binoculars, an infantry cap and a Canon DSLR camera with him. He put those into a 'Commando,' backpack.

He was wearing jungle khaki trousers and a faded, well used olive-green, long-sleeved safari shirt with numerous pockets.

The MG 3.9L V8 engine liked the roads, especially the winding steep roads, when driven by a highly competent and daring pair of hands.

The car hated being parked in the garage and was straining at the leash to get out on the road.

Noisy revving up, optimal brisk gear changes and smooth cornering, motivated the old beauty to come alive, especially as she knew she was in capable hands.

Screeching tyre sounds, yet no skidding and optimal distribution of the torque, without any fancy electronics, enabled this old girl to show what she was made of!

It was good old British physical mechanics at its best.

Michael reached his destination in sixty-five minutes, averaging a speed of around 40 km/hour, when the average speed would have been around 25 km/hour.

'Sembu Rest,' was situated at a higher elevation from the main

'A' road, with a dangerously steep access road of about 100 meters in length. Michael slowed down the car and changed down to first gear. 190 bhp did not have much trouble negotiating the steep angle, especially on first gear. He parked the MG next to the three-wheeler.

Piyal, his wife Menike and their eight-year-old son were there to greet him and all three of them worshipped this honorable gentleman who had helped them in numerous ways.

"Is there any specific thing you need from us?" Piyal enquired.

"No, I came to inquire about a migratory duck, Lesser Whistling duck, seen in this area, have you seen any ducks around this place?"

"No sir, but my son always goes to the river either to fish or to bathe in that rock pool."

Only a perceptive pair of eyes would have picked up the facial changes in Michael, which changed from a serious official type to a happy and relaxed one, seeing the eight-year-old boy.

"Hamu, would you like a cup of tea?"

"Yes I would love one, after that we can go to the river, if you are free."

"My son knows the pool better than me, because all the children go there, there's a very safe spot where anyone can take a river bath."

Piyal asked his son to lead the way through a foot path which was dangerously steep, down to the river. From the main road, it was a good 150-meter drop, which the little boy did in a couple of minutes, whilst Michael and Piyal took more than eight minutes to reach the river.

As this was the dry season and there was very little water in the river, there were many sand banks on the river bed. The rock pool was situated just below the end of the foot path. The foot path was only about 2 to 3 feet wide, with a thick growth of various trees, creepers, and rocks with big boulders which covered both sides.

On their way down, Michael made a good assessment of both sides of the foot path.

As soon as they reached the rock pool, he noticed three or four children diving and frolicking in the water close to the bridge, which was about 300 meters away, he also noticed two men fishing.

He took out his binoculars and started scanning the whole area as if he was looking for ducks.

However, his attention was actually on the fishermen with rods. He took out the camera which was fitted with a 600 mm telephoto lens. Carefully, he took photographs of both fishermen. After taking more photographs with a 24 mm lens he put everything back in the bag.

"Piyal, there are no ducks here, it's a dead rope given to me by an ornithologist, let's go back, I am wasting my time."

He pretended that he was disappointed.

However, in reality, his reconnaissance mission was a resounding success, with a thorough observation done and vital photographs taken. The added bonus was that the possible fall guys were noted and photographed.

Having enjoyed a very tasty, yet very simple lunch cooked by Piyal's wife, with organically grown vegetables from their own garden, Michael hit the road after thanking them profusely. He did not go home directly though. He drove to Kandy City, parked the car in a busy car park, took out his camera and studied the telephoto lens photographs of the two fishermen.

He memorized what they were wearing, the colors and

the hats. He had a photographic memory!

Then he took out a sports bag from the car boot, leaving the backpack inside and went to the nearby shopping mall. He went straight into the toilet and changed into a sarong, checked bush shirt, a worn-out dirty cap and put on rubber flip-flops which he had in his bag. He put the clothes he was wearing in the bag, went back to the car and left the bag in the boot.

He walked toward the market with a slouch and a limp, keeping his head bent down, while covering his face with the shade of the cap, keeping it pulled down as much as possible. He did not look up at anyone and his face was not noticeable.

He went from shop to shop, until he found sarongs and shirts somewhat similar to those worn by the fishermen but couldn't find the type of straw hats both of them were wearing.

Both sarongs were of the same design and color. He was fairly satisfied with his purchases, though he couldn't find the straw hats. He hurried back imitating the same limp, went to his car and took the sports bag from the boot, went back to the same toilet, changed back and headed toward his car.

Satisfied with his excursion, Michael came home in an elated mood.

Nicolaus noticed that the master himself was carrying both backpack and sports bag into his room; which had never happened in recent years.

Michael was elated about his cleverness and far thinking. As soon as entered the room and when he saw the map, he reached his climax and he thought that he deserved a reward.

He got the LP, 'Four Seasons,' by Vivaldi and played it on the Philips record player in his room.

Dancing away the rhythm, still only focusing on the village that he intended to visit sooner or later, he thought his crusade of breaking down the barrier of inferiority; overcoming this disability with flying colors and coming out triumphantly, was not that far away.

With the successful termination of the first adventure, he knew the second one was also going to be difficult or may even be an impossible task, if he were to survive and become a veteran at this game of intrigue.

He knew meticulous planning and precise implementation was of paramount importance in achieving success. There was no place for loose ends and a plan B must be thought of. He had only one deficiency of not being in possession of a fisherman's straw hat.

He knew he had plenty to do the following day, so he went to bed early.

In the morning, he took out his Remington seven-thousand-four-hundred rifle with its original iron sights and a box of 30, 06 cartridges. He took the canvas hunting bag with the 'across the chest' strap and stuffed it with the sarongs and shirts he had bought in Kandy town. On top of it, he laid the gun cloth, hiding the clothes and kept the cartridge box well hidden.

"Appu I am going hunting today, ask Banda to saddle 'Doodle.'

When he came near the stables 'Red Rum' was ready, saddled up. The left-handed rifle holster was hanging by the left side of the mare, since he was a left-hander.

'Doodle,' was ecstatic seeing her master and reared up on both front legs, as if she were about to clear a hedge in a steeplechase and demonstrated her excitement with an ear-splitting neigh.

"Calm down girl, this is just a preparation, you and I are going to have a lot of adventures together." He hugged the mare.

After inserting the rifle muzzle first, into the holster, he mounted 'Doodle' with ease.

After adjusting the hunting bag across his torso, "Ok girl, you and I are going to that Samuel Baker guy's hunting lodge today."

She acknowledged that with a low-pitched nicker, as if she was courting a stallion! Reaching the hunting lodge was not possible on horseback. Michael dismounted part way. "Don't run away with a stallion, I'll be back soon."

She looked at him with a suspicious face,

'Why did he have to dismount in the middle of nowhere?'

He had to negotiate a height of about 50 meters with an angle of about 70 degrees. It was the side of the rock face, which was overgrown with trees and plenty of creepers. With the help of the creepers and bushes, he managed to reach the top.

It was a flat area on top of the big rock, a 'mini plateau,' with a spectacular view down below. "Why haven't I come here before?" he regretted that he had never come here. At the same time, he was happy no one else knew such a place existed.

He sat on the rock and emptied the shoulder hunting bag on to the rock. Then he saw a little collection of dark straw colored stagnant water in a depression on the rock. He soaked the sarongs and shirts in that water and let them absorb everything for about fifteen minutes. Taking the wrinkled and soiled clothes out of the dirty water, he rubbed them roughly on the rock, to make them appear old and used.

Then rubbed everything on an anthill thoroughly. Satisfied with the appearance of the garments, he spread them out and let them dry on the rock itself.

Then he realized that he had left the rifle still in the holster. He climbed down, walked back to the mare, picked up the rifle and the cartridge box, walked back and carefully climbed up again.

Only then did he notice that the remnants of the so called 'hunting lodge,' was buried under a heavy growth of greenery.

In one area, he realized there was a wall about four feet high, though it was completely covered with vegetation. It was about four feet thick as well. He climbed on to it with the greatest difficulty, since he had the rifle with him.

He was quite surprised to see the area he could visualize from this vantage point.

It made him realize how clever and adventurous the colonial masters of Ceylon were. He was scanning the area to look for game. Not even five minutes later, he noticed some movement down below.

Initially, he couldn't see anything and then they emerged! A family of wild hogs rummaging through the ground.

There were two adults and about twelve shoats. He aimed at the biggest hog and he had a clear sighting.

Again, he thought it was unfair to shoot an animal who didn't know it was going to die, being shot from a distance.

As a matter of fact, even while a tear drop started draining down his cheek, he pressed the trigger. The animal just fell down instantly and the rest of the hogs, with various tones of squeals and squeaks, disappeared from sight.

Michael felt so sad for having just killed a hapless animal. He sat down and started crying after throwing the rifle a few feet away.

About half an hour later, he picked up the rifle, climbed down the same way he came up, leaving the clothes on the rock.

He walked up to the carcass to inspect it. As the animal had been facing away from him, the bullet had entered the skull just behind the right ear with a clean hole, but the exit wound was a mess. The opposite eye ball was lying a few feet away with part of the maxillary bone.

Michael couldn't bear the sight of it, and with tearful eyes, he picked up the carcass. It was rather heavy.

As soon as he came near Red Rum, she got agitated.

"Calm down girl, we are going back, I have to send this to our estate workers." Michael always distributed any game he bagged, among his work force.

On this occasion, it was a diversionary tactic he used, so no one would ever guess the real purpose of his visit to the Hunting Lodge.

"My girl, we have more exciting excursions lined up once I get the straw hat and an old slipper. You know, just one slipper will do. We are going to venture out to places you have never been before; I know you like water and sandbanks. Let's hope there won't be any rain soon. I promise you that will be very exciting, I don't want to disappoint you"

A low-pitched nicker from Red Rum signified a reassurance to Michael.

CHAPTER 13

"Madam, from next Monday, the Medical Faculty summer holidays begin, are you going abroad? It is a two months' vacation."

"Thank you, Trish, I had forgotten all about it completely!

No, I haven't planned anything this time. Since my father's death, I did not even get a chance to be with my mother. I thought I'll stay at the estate with my mother for a while."

Only then did she realize that since her acquaintance with Ranga, she had completely erased every other interaction with society and she was quite happy about it.

It made her think this was 'falling in love,' in a psychologist's perspective. Such analysis could be appreciated only by someone in the same line of work.

Her endorphins started to flow like a dormant waterfall suddenly come alive. A sense of euphoria touched every corner of her body, overwhelming her thought process.

Plans, Plans and yet more plans, on how to consolidate her position. She got the 'window period,' she needed on a platter and she promised herself 'it's now or never,' which even the great Elvis wouldn't have realized.

That evening, Anita stepped into Aunt Rose's abode, "Aunty Rose, I am going to the estate for a few weeks, it's my summer holiday, you'll be lonely here, would you like to join me?"

"Ooh darling, that's very sweet of you, I'd love to come!"

She hugged Anita so intensely that she couldn't breathe and

her doting mind thought, 'This old bat is bloody strong,' but she stopped short of verbalizing it.

The Jeep was almost full and ready to go.

Then Anita saw her maid, Tharanga, dragging a humongous, wheeled piece of luggage toward the jeep. She kept the luggage near the jeep and virtually ran back again toward Aunt Rose's house. Anita just watched, somewhat baffled.

'There comes another even larger piece of luggage', Anita never thought it was possible to manufacture such a big suitcase.

'However, the Jeep Wrangler is geared for such an assault with Rough Country suspension,' thought Anita.

A complete re-arrangement of baggage ensued!

Then came Dame Rose Wickramasooriya, with her attire fit for a Royal audience! She was wearing a Nova Tiered maxi and a matching scarf.

She looked so elegant that Anita thought her Wrangler jeans and Nike T-shirt was out of place, to sit with her dear Aunt.

Aunt Rose exceeded herself with Tom Ford Rive d'Ambre Eau de Parfum spray.

Probably, that was the most expensive thing which sat on that passenger seat of this modified jeep!

The rough leather seats of the jeep, meant for water, mud and whatever nature could throw at it, might have been confused as to why it had to carry something like a delicate flower and pheromone fragrance, when it was supposed to tolerate the bog.

Nevertheless, the Jeep didn't mind as long as it was not parked in a carport, in Colombo 7. The AT tyres were not very considerate of this flower though.

The Wrangler thought to itself,

'Baby this time I'll take you where you have never been before, and I'll show you my mettle!' The Jeep was enjoying every inch of the journey, especially the rough spots on the road.

Both of them didn't say much during the journey, perhaps they knew there was plenty of time to catch up with each other later. Helen was ecstatic to see her sister-in-law after many moons!

They hugged each other as if they were going for the Guinness book of World Records. Anita just watched them hugging to their hearts' content, with tears in her eyes.

However, she was worried that she had to tackle the Herculean task of unloading the 'Light Traveler's,' luggage.

However, knowing her sister-in-law Rose, Helen was prepared for such a scenario, a deck hand was ready for unloading the goodies, relieving Anita of her anxieties.

Helen had so much to tell Anita, and she thought all the good deeds she had done throughout her life, had started paying her back. She felt the time had come to; 'Let go of worldly possessions' as per Lord Buddha's teachings. She was determined to sort out all family affairs and if she succeeded, probably go to a monastery and spend the 'evening time,' of her life peacefully, devoid of any commitments.

Rose was very pleased to be with Helen, since both of them always felt somewhat strangers to the 'Wickramasooriya,' clan, even though Rose was actually one of them.

However, Helen was of the opinion that Rose was hiding some family secret which she never divulged to her.

Three beacons of the triangle of 'family secrets,' came together after all these years.

It was necessary that all three of them divulged whatever they knew for the benefit of one another. Anita knew it was Aunt Rose who could contribute the most, to relieve the other two's misery.

Rose also realized it was time to divulge everything she knew, so her conscience would be clear and to depart this world as a free human being.

The sentiment was in effect, the same for all three of them and they knew it. All three of them felt very close to each other at this decisive moment.

After dinner, Anita opened her late father's liquor cabinet full of classy drinks. Her eye caught the bottle of Louis XIII Cognac, which was her father's favorite.

The other two acknowledged Anita's choice with a nod in unison, though Helen herself, was not an avid drinker. She got the Bohemia Crystal Brandy glasses and handed them over. Then the bottle was passed around. `

Parmesan cheese and a box of water cracker biscuits, found its way to the coffee table.

The stage was set. The actors were present. No director, no script and above all, no audience!

As a matter of fact, all three themselves, were the actors, the script, the directors and even the audience, all in one!

All of them knew this was not a 'to be or not to be,' event.

Sticking to the expression 'age before beauty', Rose opened the line of fire.

However, she had to first absorb the aroma of the fine brandy sloshing in her glass, A little sip followed by a nibble on the parmesan and a piece of cracker, which ritual was followed faithfully by the other two, was the order of the night.

The play began.

"Helen and Anita, I must confess, I have been hiding some family secrets all these years, I think it is high time the truth be told. By this, I think I'll be betraying George. Nevertheless, tonight I am going to get it off my chest.

One could hear the silence so loudly, even the cracker inside the mouth created a massive audible disturbance.

Probably no one had ever seen such interactive humans on this planet, as on that night. Looking at Anita, "Your grandparents, that's mine and your father's parents Josephina and Stanislaus, had three children. Your father was the eldest and there was another brother three years younger to him and many years later, seven years later to be precise, I was born.

I was never told; I had another brother, until fairly recently, a few years before your father passed away.

That must have been the very reason, I was educated in Colombo, because they did not want me to know that I had another brother. I think Helen knows about this because your father had told your mother after your birth, when they had a party to celebrate the event.

However, your father did not divulge the exact truth, only part of it was revealed to your mother. Anita noticed an expression of betrayal creeping into her mother's face.

Rose continued, "my brother had been a difficult child and at a brawl he had pushed a boy over a cliff and that boy had died due to the fall. That much your mother was told, not the rest of it. All these, even I didn't know at all, until your father told me a few years back before his death, as I said earlier. It was all ears. The story teller par excellence with juicy fillings, held the stage."

"Your mother was told that he disappeared that day and was never to be seen again and therefore, presumed dead.

That was not what had happened exactly. Apparently, there was a rumor those days that Edward – that's his name, was not actually your father's but an Arabian horse breeder's son, the outcome of an unfortunate clandestine affair.

Your grandmother loved him very much, and he had been

hiding in a few places, till eventually he was given a different name and a passport and sent to UK for many years; and had come back with yet another different name.

Your grandmother had inherited a huge estate herself from her parents, on the other side of the nature reserve, and it had been written in his new name.

He is still living there with the bogus identity. This was revealed to your father, because Edward and George were very close to each other. As a matter-of-fact, Edward was always defending your father when the school children were bullying him."

In spite of the complications in parenthood, there had been an unbreakable bond between them.

"Anita, my clandestine excursions every now and then for days without notice, were to see my brother. I know you thought he was my lover. He is the one who was sending me money all these years, not the imaginary friend."

There was complete silence which none of the dictionaries could describe. "Now my heart and head are free,"

Rose looked at the ceiling and raised both her hands as if she were worshipping the one above.

"Forgive me George, I decided that the correct thing is to tell them the truth." She poured another stiff one and gulped it down in one go!

Washing her sins away?

Within the next few minutes, all three of them were hiding in their own cocoons of silence, trying hard to digest this revelation.

CHAPTER 14

DIG Silva was about to start the briefing. Only Police Officers were present. It was a Sunday and no one was really happy to be there in the incident room at one p.m. To some, it was hard earned 'siesta time,'

SI Pathirana felt this meeting was the DIG's ego-driven need to show who was in control and to prove that the good old 'board' was the way forward, in comparison to PowerPoint presentations.

However, Ranga respected the experience of the DIG and knew the 'board,' was a far more superior tool when it came to the 'multi-disciplinary' approach.

Instead of the 'laser pointer', the DIG preferred the long cue 'pointer stick.'

"We have to investigate all the angles possible, still we don't know what we are dealing with. As of now, what we want to know is, was it a revenge killing over a dispute, on the assumption 'how could someone hurt a child in revenge'?

So, that possibility can be ruled out. It appears that this crime was committed by some kind of a mentally deranged person. Do you all agree with me?"

The nodding of their heads in unison, confirmed the DIG's way of thinking was realistic.

"We have to go back to this child's home area and look out for abnormal personalities and drug addicts in that neighborhood. We must get information from the Grama Seva

Niladhari also. We must check people in all construction sites, transport lorry drivers, boarders and any newcomers to that area."

"Excuse me Sir, we can even ask the environmental police in that area, they have close contact with the local community" SI Pathirana chipped in helpfully.

All the facts relevant to the case, were clipped on the board by way of little 'sticky notes.' It was methodically arranged according to geographical locations, reported incidents, forensic reports and interpretations.

However, Ranga's mind was elsewhere, absorbed in thinking about Anita, her mother and Aunt Rose.

Then he noticed a WPC coming inside the incident room, almost running in and even without saluting the DIG, saying something in his ear secretively. The DIG whose face took on a serious look, nodded at Ranga and indicated to him to follow him. Then SI Pathirana noticed that nobody was listening to him due to this disturbance,

"Carry on SI," and the DIG stood up and walked out of the incident room followed by the SSP, like a duckling following its mother.

"Apparently, there's another child murdered on the other side of the reserve!" "From here, it is more than 80 km, sir" Ranga said to the DIG.

"Get the Air mobile, Ranga." "Yes Sir,"

Ranga saluted his superior and headed toward the radio room. Since there was no helipad at the Central Province Police headquarters, the Bell 206 L4 Long Range helicopter which belonged to the disaster management unit of the Air-Force, had to land on the nearest football ground.

This was the very first time both of them used this method of transportation to visit a crime scene site. The ear splitting, air chopping sounds of the 10.16-meter diameter rotor of the helicopter, was subdued only by the 'over the ear' headphones.

However, the inexperienced Police Officers did not hear anything that the pilot said to them throughout the journey, though both of them pretended they heard everything.

They were flying over the Nature Reserve. Ranga could see the tortuous river with many sand banks, boulders, rocks and an emaciated, snaky water line.

Within forty-five minutes, they reached their destination. Ranga had a 'bird's eye view,' of the Police jeeps parked on the main 'A' road, the bridge, the collection of water on a kind of rock formation and a lot of police activity near the water. The pilot said something to them, though they still didn't understand a thing.

Then the pilot flew the 'chopper,' over the bridge and turned back, keeping the nose down and pointed toward the only possible landing site, which was a fairly big sand bank in the middle of the river. Sign language got the message across and in unison, both officers gave the thumbs up simultaneously, indicating it was OK to disembark from the helicopter, on to the sand.

As soon as the chopper landed, they removed the headphones which had made both of them virtually deaf and keeping their hands on the caps, jumped on to the sand.

The pilot kept the 'low autorotation mode,' to minimize the sand dispersion while both of them walked out as quickly as possible, though a few grains of sand still managed to get into their eyes.

Even though they were a good ten meters away from the helicopter, as soon as the pilot increased the throttle to lift off, a cloud of sand engulfed both of them, covering them completely as if they were camouflaged.

As if emerging out of a sand storm in the Sahara, virtually covered in fine sand, both of them looked at the Helicopter which was gaining height and flying away from them.

Like two cats shedding ash from their fur, these two high ranking officers started shaking their bodies to get rid of the sand. Ranga couldn't see a thing and the DIG too was virtually blind!

Then they realized they were marooned on a sandy island and had to negotiate a shallow column of water about 6 inches deep and about 10 feet wide. Ranga bent down and with cupped hands collected some river water which was crystal clear and washed his face. Watching this, the DIG followed suit.

There were about fifteen Police personnel from various departments.

The OIC came forward and saluted both superior officers.

"The body is still there. We are awaiting the Magistrate and the JMO. It's an eight-year-old local boy. His house can be seen from here, that little hotel up there."

He pointed his finger above the main road, about 100 meters up.

"Two children have seen the murderer. The suspect is probably one of two fishermen who regularly fish with rods from that boulder near the bridge. We have already cordoned off the area and arrested one of them. The other one who is supposed to be a drug addict, is missing. I am sure we can get him soon. We have set up check points 15 and 30 kilometers away from both sides. All vehicles are being searched. The OIC concluded his account of the incident.

However, neither of these officers appeared to be interested. "Can you show us the body?"

"Yes Sir, come with me, it is by the side of that foot path

about 50 meters up."

The body was lying by the side of the footpath near a boulder. It was covered with a white bed sheet. As soon as they came there, a PC removed the sheet and stood to attention.

The body was lying on its stomach but the face was facing the sky. The eyes were half open and the body appeared very peaceful. His head had been rotated exactly 180 degrees.

Even though the DIG was somewhat disturbed by the sight, Ranga appeared calm and quiet. Ranga inspected the surrounding areas for any clues.

A temporary incident room had been set up on the premises of the child's home front garden, which was the 'Sembu Restaurant.'

The mother of the child, who had collapsed after seeing the body, was taken to the hospital and the Father was in a catatonic state, making him unable to speak coherently and with a permanent gaze, without any response whatsoever.

The consensus was that he too needed hospitalization and psychiatric help. Maybe they were in such a state of oblivion that they may even have forgotten to inform their benefactor.

There were two children who had witnessed the crime at very close range. Ranga knew it would be these two children who had all the information they needed. He observed that out of the fifteen police personnel, not even one female was present. With previous experience, he knew that to interview these two children, the best bet would be females.

He entered the temporary marquee set up in front of the victim's house. The DIG was already sitting there.

"Ranga, why not we ask that professor to come if she's available?

In my career of nearly forty years, this is the weirdest case I have come across!" When the DIG himself volunteered to get Anita for the inquiry, Ranga felt relieved. However, he pretended otherwise.

"Yes Sir, I'll see whether she can help us. Sir, we need a couple of WPCs here to interview the children. None of us must interview them." A nod indicated he approved that.

Ranga came out and rang Anita's mobile. He was expecting another earful, but was pleasantly surprised at the tone she talked to him.

"Oh officer, at last you remembered the professor? I missed you. I know you are busy."

"Anita, some serious development; we are on the other side of the reserve, at the 'Sembu Restaurant,' premises. A little boy has been murdered. The DIG wants you here to interview the witnesses who happen to be children. I'll see whether I can arrange a chopper."

As it was a Sunday, almost all the villagers were gathered at the nearby school premises. Then the helicopter appeared over the mountain and all the PC's got excited and started clearing the playground. Two Police jeeps were parked on the road nearby.

Three Honda 950 cc motorbikes with front protector bars, flashing blue lights and white pannier bags, ridden by young SIs wearing sunglasses, made it look like the President of Sri Lanka was arriving.

It looked like a scene from a 'film shoot.' One could say the whole village had come to a standstill and opportunistic mobile food sellers made a killing out of the mainly morbidly curious 'rubbernecks' who had converged on the scene in their numbers.

The helicopter landed with a deafening noise, toppling

plastic garbage bins nearby and sending a swarm of plastic bags and paper up in the air like in a mini tornado, augmented by dust and smoke from its exhaust.

The 'tornado,' died. There she appeared!

The lone celebrity, wearing wrangler jeans, a baggy cream-colored see-through silk blouse, blue lensed black tapering sunglasses and brown leather ankle-length cowboy boots, though neither gun nor horse was in sight!

The young police officers couldn't take their eyes off her and eagerly volunteered to show her the way; so much so, that even the famous crooner, Frank Sinatra, may not have been able to show her his way.

Anita was somewhat disappointed when a young SI came forward to greet her, instead of the SSP himself.

However, she changed her mind after she saw the escort with sirens and blue flashing lights, making her look like a VIP!

The DIG and the SSP were there to greet her personally at the temporary incident room set up in front of the victim's house.

She was very pleased when she saw that the corner of the marquee was separated and on a desk were placed some sweets, biscuits and cans of soft drinks, with a few chairs placed in a circular formation.

"Professor, thank you very much for coming at such short notice. For our luck, I believe you were with your mother nearby. As Officer Fernando suggested, we have arranged your interview area. Two WPC's will be there to help you."

The DIG himself showed her the set up.

Ranga was shadowing the DIG and Anita pretended Ranga didn't exist.

All the men left the area. This was to be a recorded interview which could be produced in a court of law. SSP Ranga came in front of the camera and briefed about the date, location, time and officials present and their designations. A board showing an AIB number was shown.

Only Anita and a WPC with a laptop, were left at the scene. A few moments later, another WPC came with two little boys aged six and eight. First, they were asked to help themselves to the treat and told that they were filming this; and then a microphone was set up. The only male present, the cameraman, stayed behind the camera. Both boys were asked to sit side by side and the cameraman placed a high-definition microphone in front of the boys. Then both of them were asked to state their names and the voice levels were adjusted.

One WPC started asking general introductory questions and then the relevant questions began.

"Malith, you are the one who saw what happened properly, can you describe it from the beginning?" Malith was hesitant to say anything and Anita realized the little boy was petrified.

"I think this approach is not correct, we have to stop it."

Ranga saw Anita coming out and was puzzled as to why she was walking out. "Why what happened?"

"They are too scared; I don't think this is proper. Do you think we can find two voice recorders, the ones used by secretaries?"

DIG Silva got up from his chair which was kept under a turpentine tree. "Any problem Professor?"

"I think this method is not suitable, we have to send these two boys to their homes and ask their mothers to ask them what had happened and for them to record it, then they might feel free to talk. So, we need two voice recorders to be given to them and their parents briefed on what to ask. Everything has to be done through 'trial and error.'"

"Good suggestion, Professor!"

Ranga asked SI Pathirana to bring both sets of parents and to hand the children over to them. The parents of both boys were nearby, waiting anxiously. One Father said he could record it from his mobile but the other boy's parents did not have a phone with a recording facility. A voice recorder was brought and the parents were trained on how to operate it. They were briefed on what to ask by the SI and were told during the course of the day, to leisurely ask the boys what had happened and to record their narrations. Then they were sent home.

The DIG came and apologized to Anita, saying they had wasted her time and asked the OIC of that area to drop the professor home.

"We have to move this to the local police station."

After giving the order, the DIG and SSP Fernando got into the police jeep and proceeded toward the local police station.

By this time, Anita was being transported back to her home.

On her way back home, which was approximately thirty kilometers away, Anita drifted into a world of her own and the photograph of the victim she had seen frightened her.

She was trying to fit this personality to a standard text-book description but she was nowhere near finding this particular one. She needed to do a literature search.

However, she felt the mobile was not the answer to that search.

Then she saw Ranga's text thanking her and apologizing for not being able even to speak to her. She felt she must let him do his job and regretted going back to the incident room that day, assuming it was a mistake and had made Ranga a 'laughing stock' among the officers.

She wanted to send a text apologizing, but she changed her mind.

In the meantime, at the police station, Ranga went through the statement of the fisherman arrested. He found his alibis were quite 'watertight' and asked them to release him.

By this time, an angry crowd was gathering in front of the police station and he came to know that the houses of these two fishermen were stoned. He immediately ordered police protection for both houses!

The fisherman who had disappeared, was still absconding and three search parties were employed to comb the nature reserve. Around three p.m., the teams allocated to the crime site returned without any signs of success. The Inspector who was in charge of these teams made the first briefing, with possible items related to the crime being pinpointed.

"Sir, we traced the path this murderer took, because it was easy due to trampled bushes, twisted little branches and fallen fresh leaves. It appears this person had come and gone along the same path to the river. He had taken a very difficult path through the thick jungle and reached the river about one kilometer away.

We found this single, well worn-out rubber slipper on this track, about one hundred meters away from the victim. The strange thing is, at the river bank there were a lot of strange footmarks within a radius of about 10 meters but nothing else. Our conclusion was that the murderer followed the water stream by wading in it. We went about three kilometers up and down but couldn't find any place where this person would have come out.

Very strange!

The footprints are big and not like cattle or buffalo. We

photographed everything. We are sending the slipper to the Government analyst for a report."

"Thank you, can you get these footprints on to a big screen?"

"Sorry Sir, we don't have a projector or a big screen."

"That's OK, can you email that to me?"

"Yes Sir!" He saluted his SSP and the DIG and left.

"Ranga, I think we have to head back to my office, would you like to join me?" "Yes Sir!"

Later, it was rumored that the funeral of the boy had taken place with the help of a substantial contribution by an anonymous philanthropist!

CHAPTER 15

Anita was going through the backgrounds of reported psychopaths like, Charles Manson, Jack the Ripper, Albert fish, Ted Bundy, Ed Gein and a few others.

Their profiles had certain similarities with this one but Anita couldn't pinpoint anything specific which was of relevance. Nowhere were twisted necks recorded!

There was one thing clear though, he was bound to strike again.

This looked very much like a serial murder with the likelihood of it being repeated. Anita was in a dilemma as to whether she should get involved with this solely for the sake of academic reasons or whether she should exert more weight on finding this particular psychopath.

In Sri Lanka, there was no data base at all in that respect, as far as she knew.

She was not finding anything which could be applied constructively to the profiling of this psychopath, so she abandoned the idea. She knew Ranga was busy and she must not disturb him.

In this backdrop, she thought it would be better to acquaint herself with her mother more, which was overdue by a lifetime; since that was the purpose of this visit anyway.

She saw Aunt Rose was very relaxed and enjoying the climate, the scenery, the serene atmosphere and above all, her relative Helen, with whom she has had somewhat of an estranged relationship so far.

Both of them shared a similar mindset which gave prominence to 'forgive and forget,' and make up once and for all. Now they made up for lost opportunities. They became very close and shared many a secret.

It was a sunny Monday morning with clear blue skies, a soothing gentle breeze and various birds chirping away happily.

After lunch, Anita sat on a reclining chair called 'Hansi Putuwa,' in Sinhala, on the verandah; overlooking the distant mountain range, where on the other side was the nature reserve. She just realized how serene life here was and she was glad her mother had decided to stay in this 'haven' and indulge in the beauty of it. She was feeling a bit sleepy after the heavy meal she had.

"Anita, would you like a toffee?"

There she was, Aunt Rose holding a circular tin of toffees. She just got up from her slumber, put out her hand and took one. With sleepy eyes, she opened the wrapper and put the toffee straight into her mouth. Whilst enjoying the sweet, she fell asleep on the recliner.

About one hour later, she suddenly got up to the chime of the Grandfather's clock. Three chimes. So, it was three o'clock in the afternoon!

Someone from the kitchen "Would you like a cup of tea?" She was lazy to get up.

Magilin the cook, came with a tray complete with a Royal Albert New Country Roses, 'Formal Vintage,' tea pot with matching cups and saucers. She laid the tray on the cast iron table and arranged the chairs in front of the verandah in the front garden, on the well-maintained lawn.

"'Chuti Menike, tea is ready."

When Anita got up from the recliner, from the corner of her eye, she noticed something falling and the color seemed familiar to her.

It was a colorful toffee wrapper. Her heart stopped.

"This color is in my mind, Oh my Goood," an extra vowel or two.

"This was very similar to the wrappers found near the crime scene and inside the reserve."

She virtually ran toward Rose who was coming toward the lawn to have a cup of tea with her.

"Aunty Rose, from where did you get those toffees?"

"Why, are they not good?" Puzzled, Rose looked at her with a somewhat denying attitude. "Tell me from where did you get it?" "Are these available in Sri Lanka?"

Without answering Rose's question, Anita kept on asking a barrage of questions which made Rose annoyed.

"What's up Anita, why are you so agitated over a toffee?"

Only then did Anita realize she was overreacting and apologized.

"You know Anita, I love sweets; I bought these in Indonesia with that coffee and nuts. I brought five tins."

"Is this available in Sri Lanka?" "As far as I know, it is not."

Anita became more puzzled and thought she probably misidentified the toffee wrapper. Though in deep thought, she enjoyed the tea and decided to go for a walk to think straight but kept the wrapper. The rest of the evening, she was not settled until she took a photo of the well spread wrapper and WhatsApp it to Ranga.

"Ranga, please check this photo with those two pieces of

toffee wrappers and see if they are the same."

Though Ranga wanted to have a loving, flirty chat, she was not interested.

He was enjoying a pint at the officers' mess and Don Williams filled in as his companion for the rest of the evening, until he finished his fifth.

That evening, whilst they were having dinner, Rose asked both Helen and Anita if it was OK to invite her brother Michael to the estate.

Both of them were eagerly waiting to come to know this newly found elusive uncle and brother-in-law of theirs.

Hearing this, Helen couldn't control her emotions, since she had been suspecting this gem of a man, her late husband George, all this time.

She remembered how he held her hand gently after revealing facts about Edward, though she doubted very much that he did not divulge the exact truth. She had already forgiven George for that. It crossed her mind how protective he was of his brother, as he was protective of herself and Anita.

A few tears found their way down her cheeks, which she wiped off with her fingers. Both Rose and Anita saw this and the sentiment was mutual, though no one said a word. Rose wiped off her own tears and Anita did the same. Anita took this opportunity to hand over her father's wedding ring to her mother without much ado.

The following day at the breakfast table, Rose was all smiles. "Michael is coming this evening to stay with us for a few days."

It was exactly 4.35 in the evening when a majestic looking Rolls Royce Phantom pulled into the old-fashioned open car port covered with a tiled roof. The intimidating wrangler jeep and the majestic Rolls Royce side by side, were a sight to see and gave this ancient mansion the sophisticated look it deserved.

One could see a very handsome and smiling personality getting down from the car with much confidence and pausing, looking at the three ladies waiting for him.

Needless to say, it was the tearful Rose who rushed forward and embraced this fine specimen of a male.

"Helen, this is my brother Michael, Michael this is your sister-in-law Helen." Having first curtsied to Helen, Michael looked at Anita attentively.

"I presume you are Anita, my niece whom I have never met, though I know everything about you."

Anita liked him instantly and regretted that destiny punished people this way, by keeping them from getting to know each other all these years.

She didn't see her father in him, probably her mind was conditioned after Aunt Rose's revelation. She was trying to grasp as much about him as possible, then realized he had her mother's kindly eyes. Apparently, she had got it from her grandmother.

The nose, forehead, eye brows and ears were definitely of an Arabian extract. The voice was distinctly foreign, as was hers, though she thought to start with, she may be biased.

Helen was highly taken up by her brother-in-law whom she had never seen before and came forward and hugged and kissed him as if they were known to each other for years; and were meeting after many years of separation.

However, Anita was somewhat reluctant to embrace this stranger she had only been acquainted with a few moments ago.

"Professor, you are not sure about your uncle, are you?"

Michael rescued Anita from embarrassment and kissed her hand very gently with a slight bowing posture, usually done in the presence of Royalty.

Anita thought what a perfect gentleman he was and regretted she hadn't hugged him.

Pleasantries were exchanged and introductions completed. Michael went toward the car to see the deck hands already waiting for his instructions. When she saw the much smaller version of Aunt Rose's luggage coming out of the boot of the Rolls, she thought it ran in the 'Wickramasooriya,' family; even the physical artefacts.

Michael was the star of the moment. Once in the sitting room, he poured out a Brandy Alexander all round, showing his superiority in entertaining visitors, by bend de cacao with another chocolate liqueur he found in George's liquor cabinet, even though he was a visitor himself.

What was it after all? Home from home! The 'Alexanders,' perked up the trio. Alcohol levels were climbing up way beyond a breathalyzer could measure and would have even intoxicated the breathalyzer itself.

Then came the music with George's, Linn Sondek LP12 Turntable being brought to life after a lapse of about fifteen years, by courtesy of his own long-lost brother.

The 'Blue Danube Waltz,' flowing slowly and picking up on tempo, was the breaking point for both Rose and Anita, yet Rose did beat Anita to the floor with Michael, to be rudely interrupted soon after by Anita, with a rather persuasive,

"May I?"

Helen was tapping her feet to the beat, reminiscing hers and George's youthful days.

The queen of waltz, Rose, was comprehensively beaten by the princess of jive and twist Anita, when Chubby Checker's 'Let's twist again,' and Jerry Lee Lewis's 'Great Balls of Fire,' started to rain on them.

However, Helen surprised both of them with a classical Foxtrot, 'Cheek to Cheek,' with Louis Armstrong, displacing both of them who were feeling out of place in that arena, comprehensively! Thereby, Michael established his versatility in the art of Dancing as well!

Even the pair of Spot-Bellied Eagle-Owls feeding in the nearby Jak tree, took time out to watch this spectacular display of human behavior.

Civet cats, mongooses, even frogs, were enjoying the music and cavorting, keeping time with the beat. However, the snakes were in a dilemma as they were sans feet; but they too improvised with a rhythmic writhing movement.

This exuberant display went on till the wee hours of the next morning. That was the night the nocturnal creations of God in the neighborhood, stuffed to the gills with this mini-extravaganza, went hungry!

At the breakfast table set up on the front lawn the following day, everyone felt a sense of belonging and being wanted. It was a beautiful commencement of a friendship and companionship by courtesy of the long – lost son of Philomena and Stanislaus!

Michael became very close to both Helen and Anita alike. He discussed matters pertaining to the management of such vast real estate, labor management and tax affairs. All three ladies were very impressed with his knowledge about these matters, Anita felt he was teaching her how to take over the estates and she felt grateful to him.

For chivalry and charm, he would have made Omar Sharif look like a novice! Was this a Jekyll and Hyde character in real life?

The friendship per se, was a bond welded in steel!

CHAPTER 16

Helen's Mercedes S class driven by Tudor the driver, reached the British built 'open deck,' design Iron bridge which was exactly one hundred and thirty-two years old, near the 'Sembu Restaurant'. There were three white flags hung over the entrance road of the restaurant.

The whole area was in a somber mood, even the usually talkative crows were in mourning. The morning Cacophony of Squirrels had all gone silent, though the 'bad omen,' piercing cry of the 'Ulama,'known as the Devil Bird or Spot Bellied Owl, was at its highest pitch.

No river bathers, no fishermen and even the egrets had abandoned the area, due to fear of this killer.

"*Ammi*, this the place that horrible murder happened," "Atrocious," Rose said in a strong British accent.

Helen just looked at the restaurant. Everybody entered their own cocoons of thoughts and analyzed this enigma on their own biased way. Nobody spoke. Anita however, was trying to get into the shoes of this psychopath to try and help the police.

Since she was an expert on voice analysis, she thought at least one phone call from this psychopath to the police, as it happens in films, would have given some indication to her. When she was getting rather frustrated, she felt the car slowing down and the driver asking,

"Madam, is it close to the estate?"

"It's rounded the next corner, the board is there, it says 'Cline

Lower Estate.'

When Aunt Rose said this, Anita realized that no one had spoken a single word for more than one and a half hours since they had passed the murder site.

The location of the estate and the ideal 'picture post card,' view of a 'mountain range scenery,' would have taken landscape photographers into their own world of ultimate bliss.

Anita and Helen were mesmerized by the view and Helen felt somewhat envious in a positive way, since her brother-in-law had a better place to live. However, Rose who had visited her brother's estate regularly in the past, felt as if she were going home, this time with the whole clan of Wickramasooriyas.

There he was, probably the oldest eligible bachelor in the central province, or even maybe the whole of Sri Lanka, waiting for the three ladies; wearing a Scottish Shetland pure woolen trouser, a Pima cotton white shirt, a cardigan of the same Shetland brand and a matching Scottish Tam hat.

He looked like an urbanized Scottish Warrior, sans the beard.

Needless to say, the ladies were quite impressed with his dress sense, augmented by his welcoming mannerism. Appu asked Banda to take the luggage to the two visitors' rooms prepared especially for this occasion.

Anita and Helen shared a room.

Banda, liked madam Anita instantly and Anita too felt the same.

The breakfast table was ready on the humongous balcony. Everyone was admiring the view from this vantage point and Helen felt her front garden view was useless comparatively.

So, it is how one's mind works, proving the idiom that 'the grass is greener on the other side of the hedge.'

Anita walked the entire length of the balcony admiring the

view, absorbing every little bit of beauty before her, like dried mud absorbs the rain drops.

Michael had to remind these beauties that breakfast was being served.

Stereotyped Appu, who had acquired a stiff upper lip learning while serving his master, never liked the Madam Rose.

Dutiful Appu who had a wealth of experience in butler duty, was very saddened and dismayed when Madam Rose always found fault with him. Being a submissive personality to his master, Appu felt very much dejected in the presence of Madam Rose.

However, he saw the kind eyes of Madam Helen and he sensed she wanted to know about his master. He felt obliged to share a few secrets with her about his master and wasn't sure if he would get the opportunity.

Anita was feeling lonely even though she was with the best company she could have thought of. She felt something was missing.

Then she realized it was Ranga who was the missing link.

"Hey Officer, leave that psychopath alone and come and meet some sane people, you are not that far away. I believe it is around 40 kilometers from your boring office. If you like, I can send my mother's car. We have the driver with us, what do you say? This place is so serene that we don't want any noisy contraptions disturbing the peace here," referring to his noisy bike.

Anita didn't leave any gap in this communication. The way it was presented, Ranga didn't have any choice but to comply. However, truth to tell, he was actually waiting for this invitation and he was of the opinion that since Anita went to her mother's, she was somewhat ignoring him.

"Ok Anita I can come, nothing's going to happen for a few days whilst we wait for reports, thank you very much for offering the transport, it's much appreciated, I missed you a lot"

"OK big boy, your transportation is on its way."

Ranga arrived around six thirty in the evening. He got an uneasy feeling as soon as he got down from the Mercedes, when he saw the classy mansion, the furniture and the life style of Anita's family member.

He felt, out of place and somewhat of an inferiority complex crept into his mind, making him think whether he was doing the right thing.

His thought process started torturing him and he had a feeling of anxiety on whether this was a mistake. However, he put on a brave face and pretended everything was fine.

"Uncle Michael, this is my friend SSP Ranga who is conducting the investigations into those horrific murders."

'Walk into my parlor' as the spider said to the fly.

"How do you do, Officer Ranga?" Michael's grip was so strong, Ranga felt like his hand was crumbling due to the intense force.

Furthermore, Michael's penetrating eye contact was so intense, Ranga felt like a minion in front of a Hercules.

His 'inferiority infected,' mind was not helping either, to resurrect the lost pride or to face these Wickramasooriyas' aristocratic conduct. He felt so small.

When he walked in with the rest, it was not another Grandfather's clock, but a huge ebony cupboard containing trophies of stuffed animals, warrior swords and various ancient combat weapons, that were waiting to bully him.

Though at Anita's place, he challenged the lone 'Grandfather,' here, he was not in a position even to look at these animals and weapons with any degree of authority.

He wished he were blind so he would not have to go through

this agony of intimidation. However, Anita the warrior queen, was there to defend him.

That night was the night that particular balcony was put to its maximum potential though there were only five people. Of course, Aunt Rose was dressed for the occasion.

However, Anita had the necessary attire to save Ranga from embarrassment, she wore her patched denims and a white Nike dri-FIT T-shirt.

Her thirty-six-inch chest was augmented by the Body Contour T-shirt, satisfying both Anita and the T-shirt alike.

The T-shirt thanked the designers for their ingenuity and grabbed hold of everything it could.

Being a maestro in this game of entertainment, Michael played an entirely different set of songs.

He started with Swan Lake act1 Waltz followed by My Sweet and Tender Beast by Eugen Doga to lure his sister Rose onto the floor, hoping Helen and Anita would join in.

Anita saw Ranga was in a fix not knowing how to waltz; so, she took his hand and descending the spiral stairway reached the perfectly manicured lawn, with the drinks held in their other hands.

Ranga felt quite relieved and thanked her profusely for rescuing him from this predicament he was about to encounter.

Though he was waltzing away with Rose, Michael realized that the young couple was missing and acted immediately, changing the music to Beatle's Twist & Shout, followed by Chubby Checker's Dance the Mess Around, which brought this young couple virtually running back up the spiral stairs, like bullets off a rifle.

The boring Police officer was full of energy and rhythm thanks to Professor's one to one teaching in that disco full of weirdos, a few weeks back.

Good old Beatles, Chuck Berry, Jimmy Soul and many more were lined up to entertain these young and old alike.

Even Helen couldn't resist the legends of yesteryear Rock-'n'-Roll. She felt she couldn't compete with the young blood on that arena of rolling and beat every one of them, especially to take sweet revenge on Rose.

Therefore, she chose her own songs and made sure to take the only available male slave of her vintage, Michael, by herself; starting with a quickstep, a foxtrot and a much-forgotten Bolero as the icing on the cake of dances that night, beating Rose into oblivion.

That night was also a night all the animals in the vicinity had to go hungry, watching this free show. However, the Sri Lankan jackals took the opportunity to educate themselves on how to trot.

At the breakfast table, Ranga was very much relaxed.

However, what had happened in the wee hours of the morning, in the guest room which Anita and Ranga occupied, the bed, the ceiling, the wardrobe and even the walls were speechless except for the loud, squeaky ceiling fan, experiencing its own squeaky orgasm, having had a bird's eye view of the nocturnal activities below!

Everyone was in a state of bliss, augmented by Michael's communication prose.

There were so many things to do as one desired. Helen decided to pay a visit to the tea factory, Rose obviously inquired about the rose garden and the young lovers just took an aimless walk through the tea bushes.

However, Michael's eagle eyes were focused on the young police officer and he had good reason to do so.

"Ranga, how is my Uncle Michael?" She did not reveal he

146

was an elusive phantom who just appeared in their lives only a few days before.

"Oh, I like him, he is a very classy gentleman, I suppose he is a typical old school colonial specimen, we can learn a lot from them."

Ranga stopped, looked eye to eye with Anita and held her hand, "Darling I am really scared of your family and your wealth; I am no match for you. I am just a mediocre middle-class guy; I am not sure whether I belong here at all."

One could see Anita's face changing from absolute bliss into 'spiraling down surprise,' and disbelief. Ranga noticed tears slowly finding their way down her cheeks and she didn't say anything.

Ranga put his arms around her and hugged her and whispered in her ear "Darling, I am so sorry; I just simply spoke my mind."

Anita neither spoke to him nor stopped crying. It just so happened that their happy walk came to an abrupt end and she just walked back without uttering a single word, eagerly watched by the 'eagle eyes,' with his powerful telescope.

Had young Romeo learned yet another bitter lesson and regretted his words? Then again he thought, 'Oh my God I don't understand this woman.' Looking down from above, the creator himself would also have thought, 'I myself am still confused about women, this poor mortal has to come to terms with reality' and said to himself 'please leave me alone on this.'

Seeing Anita walking back fast to the house and Ranga waiting like a zombie just looking in the direction where Anita had gone, 'predator,' Michael saw his opportunity.

"Hello Ranga, I see you are alone, shall we go for a walk? I'll show you how these estates function. It is an art, this tea planting."

Ranga was surprised as to where Michael appeared from, then again he thought he needed some time out to think about women.

"Ranga, be careful don't brush against the tea bushes, Green pit vipers are common here, you don't see them easily, especially people like you who don't have the experience. Stick to the middle of the pathways."

One thing Ranga hated in this world and was scared about were the creepy crawlies. He was so alarmed, he just dashed to the middle of the gravel estate road.

Michael was a maestro in making conversation, and it didn't take even a few minutes for Ranga to take a liking to him completely and become a victim of Michael's spell. Michael instinctively knew what others wanted to hear, though he never had any education in public relations. Michael knew Ranga was feeling out of place, so he made a special effort to make him feel comfortable. They walked for about an hour and at the end of it, Ranga began to really like Michael and felt quite at home here.

He now felt like he was part and parcel of these high echelons of society. However, what he didn't realize was, he had got himself trapped in Michael's devious plans.

Though Rose was openly admiring her brother's rose patch, she covertly envied Michael's roses, since his roses were much healthier and vibrant.

Maybe it was to do with the climate, she thought. That is not to say that while she was engrossed with the roses, she was not inquisitive about what was going on with the others.

She noticed every bit of development, like Ranga and Anita's stroll, Anita dashing back to the house, Michael's reconnaissance with his telescope and when opportunity knocked, to take it; and the change of Ranga's strolling partner and eventually, Ranga the hunk, coming back in a jubilant mood.

The David Austin rose bush 'The Lady of the Lake,' herself, was very upset.

Without admiring her, this woman called Rose was watching elsewhere and ignoring her. Then again she thought 'it's another woman, who am I to argue about this?' 'The lady of the Lake,' was happy when Rose pricked her finger on one of the sharp thorns.

When exhausted, the Sun God began losing his altitude and hiding behind the knuckles mountain range, when the much hopeful nocturnal animal life took their seats; anticipating yet another spectacular human display, of which were to them, absolutely useless courting rituals.

Nevertheless, all male animals pacified themselves thinking that at least all the females would be in a receptive mood after witnessing such behavior.

Michael changed his tactics and decided to host a seven-course meal on the balcony, so he could buy time to get all the information he wanted from this police officer. It worked like magic, to the utter dismay of the nocturnal life outside, waiting eagerly to get a glimpse of these human rituals of courting.

"Ranga, you are heading the investigations into these atrocious child murders, any headway into it?" Rose opened up the conversation.

"We are still collecting data and trying to build up a profile of this killer and Anita is an immense help." Ranga looked at Anita.

"Up to now, I have not been much of a help." Anita contributed with a shy smile.

"Oh no, she is making heaps of progress, even stirring up the Police Department." with a sarcastic smile, Ranga took another sip of his Malt Whiskey and looked at Anita to see her reaction.

"Bunch of record keepers, belong to an archives room," Anita was not going to lie low.

"Be careful Ranga, Anita will drive them insane, that's what psychologists are capable of," Helen couldn't resist interjecting after sipping a few glasses of Croft Original sherry.

Everyone laughed in unison, except the ever-attentive listener, Michael.

"One thing we have established, that this killer is from this area and he is bound to strike again. Already, we have employed our mufti intelligence squad within a 50-kilometer circle."

Michael's face lit up with a smile which no one noticed. Until then he did not utter a single word.

"I think it's time to stretch our legs," Michael stood up.

This time it was a quick slow with Helen, followed by a slow dance which was really meant for Ranga and Anita, and it worked. Michael of course, held center stage with Helen and Rose. The nearby spectators were keenly watching whether there was something of importance to learn.

The bats, hanging down, had the best angle if one desired a bit of spice into a copulation ritual.

Mission accomplished! Michael did not disappoint both ladies. Whilst doing the slow dance, he was calculating his next move.

CHAPTER 17

Armed with vital pieces of intelligence, this psychopathic mind devised a cunning plan to confuse the long arm of the law. One can safely say, this deranged mind was surpassing the most intelligent human ever to be born; even making the character in Johann Wolfgang von Goethe's first novel, look like an imbecile.

He had a master plan! To implement such, he needed to lay the groundwork meticulously, and that is exactly what he did. To satisfy his morbid desires and to reach the orgasm of dominance, he needed many trophies in his bag.

He was ecstatic, since he already had two feathers in his cap of 'excellent achievement.'

He was a 'man with a mission,'! He needed a minimum of three weeks to implement his plans for the 'Mother of all Operations,' and a few months of hibernation. First thing was to formulate the master plan. So, it became his priority.

The telephone of the 'World Travel Tours,' office rang exactly at eight thirty a.m.

"I wish to book a three-week holiday in South East Asia, would you help me to organize it please? Is it possible for me to come and visit you?"

So, it was done. Dates were fixed. Full payment done in advance. Even the airport taxi was booked from his estate to the Katunayake International airport to drop him and to pick him up three weeks later, from the airport to his estate.

The following day, a tourist booked a ticket to Hikkaduwa

on the luxury tourist train from Colombo. The same tourist booked a double room for three days in a small family-run bed and breakfast. The tourist inquired whether he could hire a scooter for three days from them.

On the third day, there was a booking from a tourist from Koggala, by Aqua plane to Trincomalee. There was also a booking for a family room in yet another small hotel for five days in Trincomalee. Hotels.com showed that the hotel had surfboards, bicycles and motorcycles on hire facilities. Apparently, the same family had booked two motorcycles for local travel.

There was an intercity train booking for two persons from Anuradhapura to Jaffna, two days later. A small hotel in Jaffna had a booking for a double room for three days.

The following day, there was a flight booked from Jaffna to Ratmalana Airport.

Itinerary completed. Now he had a long list of shopping to do. Two 120-liter back packs, black leather jeans and a black leather rider's jacket, full face cover helmet, small tent, electric lantern, head torch, riders' gloves, disposable surgical gloves, various wigs and moustaches, various sunglasses and normal spectacles, a variety of hats and caps, beanies and numerous miscellaneous items used for disguising oneself.

He planned his daily routines; what he was going to wear and the disguise needed for each and every location from the day he was leaving. All these intricate details were carefully written down in a small note book. This time, for his shopping, he went to Colombo. Of course, in a disguise of sorts.

He needed a fair amount of cash, so he prematurely uplifted two of his fixed deposits in two different banks in Colombo.

He intended to pay cash for everything and set aside the

correct amounts of cash required to pay for room charges, transport etc., for each stay. He wanted to pay the room charges up front in cash, at the check-in. The money was put in separate envelopes, labelled and sealed and stored in a small bag. No credit cards were to be used.

He enjoyed all this planning and fantasized about twisting heads exactly 180 degrees.

His main desire was to see widely opened, staring eyes, a popped-out tongue and a completely flaccid body. He reminisced about his greater achievements of yesteryear, such as whole eyeballs popping out of frogs and regretted that it was not possible in humans.

Then again he pacified himself that 'One had to be satisfied with what one can achieve.' He thought he was a very reasonable man, keeping to the inherent limitations applicable.

He hung a single plate 24" x 18" road map of Sri Lanka on the wall and marked his playgrounds he was yet to annex. He demarcated possible places of attack, especially rivers, streams and small tributaries where a road intersects. Satisfied with his choice, he knew that enticing his targets would be easy, since it was away from home; and solemnly promised himself he would never try anything within at least a 150 km radius from his estate.

However, having police officer Ranga's head twisted exactly 180 degrees with popped out eyes and a flaccid uniformed body, was his supreme orgasmic aspiration!

CHAPTER 18

Anita was admiring the landscape, whilst walking through the tea estate and thinking about the wealth she was going to inherit eventually. She couldn't imagine the probable inheritance of her uncle's wealth as well, should he decide to write it to her. She definitely liked him and she felt he liked her too.

It was far too much for her to grasp, so she sat down by the gravel road and floated in and out of a cloud between an academic career in Colombo and moving to Kandy, living in this serene environment and managing the estate.

It was Aunt Rose, who made her jump by tapping on her shoulder, bringing her down to mother earth, full of opportunities and dangers alike.

Anita did appear as if she were in a trance when Aunt Rose said to her, "Darling, Uncle Michael is going on a holiday abroad for three weeks, he wants me to go to his estate and look after it in the meantime. Would you like to come with me? As a matter of fact, he thinks it would be nice for you to be there as well, since Ranga is only forty kilometers away from his estate."

Only then did she realize that she had been dreaming all this time. "Aunty, can you please repeat what you said?"

The airport limousine turned into the 'Lower Cline,' estate road. The tourist was ready, dressed in olive corduroy trousers, equally matching short sleeved Balenciaga Bahama cotton shirt and an unusual Borges & Scott Panama hat.

As expected, Anita saw the 'Wickramasooriya,' trade mark

luggage.

However, Uncle Michael's luggage was not anywhere near the size of the luggage of Aunt Rose, she thought.

Anita was so pleased when Uncle Michael hugged her and told her; "Darling, learn the trade while you are there."

When Michael was about to get into the limousine, Rose came running.

"Michael, you are not going anywhere without these, how absent minded are you?" She handed over the airline tickets, travel agent's itinerary and passport to Michael. "You have left these on the corner table where the telephone is."

"Oh, this has never happened to me before, how strange! I just confirmed my arrival to the hotel in Singapore, thank you Rose, you are an angel."

The limousine disappeared from sight while Anita was wiping away the tears. She felt really emotional though it was only a three-week tour.

With a sarcastic smile, Michael completed his first item on his list of deceiving tactics. The limousine dropped him off at the departure terminal. The driver brought him a luggage trolley and loaded his two cases of luggage on to it for which trouble, he received a handsome reward. Once the limousine left, he pushed the trolley towards arrivals. He got into a taxi and gave an address of a storage company nearby. As soon as he arrived at the storage company, he had his luggage unloaded and released the taxi.

He took out two backpacks stored inside the fancy luggage and he asked for the directions to the WC and there, he changed to a denim trouser, T-shirt, sandals and spectacles and put his tourist attire into the luggage. Then he handed over the two pieces of luggage for storage. At the gate, he called a *tuk tuk* and got in with his two backpacks.

155

As per the prior booking done, Michael checked into the hotel near the airport. As soon as he checked in, he changed the original sim card of his mobile with another one which he had purchased in Colombo, Front Street, with a bogus national ID number. Immediately, he rang the Airlines, informing them that passenger D.A.M. Warnayaka was cancelling the journey on flight number SA 203 to Singapore. Next, he called the hotel in Singapore to cancel the booking, followed by calls to the Singapore, Thailand and Malaysian travel agents handling his booked tours and did the same.

Phase two completed. He stayed inside the room and ordered food to the room and spent the night there. He ordered a taxi at six thirty a.m. the next morning, to take him to Colombo.

A tourist wearing cream colored chino pants, a bush shirt with a large floral pattern and a straw hat, carrying two back packs and who appeared to be a part of a tourist group, boarded the luxury tourist train to Hikkaduwa at eight thirty a.m. from Colombo Fort Railway Station.

In comparison to her parents' estate, Anita really liked her Uncle Michael's estate, since it was situated in a much more picturesque and salubrious environment.

She liked the balcony, especially the sunrise and sunset, which were clearly visible due to its location; having an almost 290-degree vision, except for Michael's room which obstructed the view.

Early morning, the sun emerged from behind the distant Knuckles Mountain range after hiding all night in some secret place, where even the best 'hide and seek,' champion would not have been able to seek it.

She loved the early morning 'floating mountain tops,' on low-lying thick layers of mist.

She felt that when the sun was hiding, the white mist kept all the trees and animals underneath very well protected with its ever-changing canopy, until the Sun God took over every morning.

The mist was no match for the sun rays, and went into total submission whenever the Sun God smiled over the mountains.

Only the Rain God had the guts to defeat the Sun God.

However, every now and then, a compromise was negotiated with a multicolored rainbow, where both rain and sun co-existed side by side. This was Anita's ultimate bliss of nature!

The day after her uncle left, Anita came to the balcony early morning to witness the Sunrise. She sat on the cast iron chair, still somewhat wet due to the mist. She was wearing her cotton pajamas, though she covered herself with the lilac, silk-lined, woolen robe she had bought many years ago from Bonsoir of London, to keep the morning chill away. Still, it was a soothing feeling.

She could feel the ruthless cold penetrating the four hundred – and twenty-five-pounds worth piece of garment, losing the battle to keep her buttocks and thighs warm!

She was mesmerized by the scenery before her and she inhaled a lungful of pure morning air, though her trachea, bronchi and bronchioles were not too pleased with the cold air.

From the corner of her eye, she noticed Aunt Rose struggling up the spiral stairway, to get to the open balcony.

As per human nature and the inherent sense of avarice within a Human being, one can say Anita would have been reluctant to help her dear old aunt; with the possibility that she was going to be the sole heir, in the event Aunt Rose had a fall and died.

The human mind is fickle, as such thought processes are always true to one's desires. Nevertheless, true to 'let's pretend,';

"Aunty Rose be careful, wait for me, that stairway is

slippery."

Anita came running and took Rose's hand and helped her to climb the rest of the stairs. Rose thought 'What an angel.' "Thank you, dear"

Whilst sitting, both of them were admiring the sunrise which was indicating that yet another day had dawned for all living creatures to enjoy.

"I wonder what Uncle Michael would be doing at this very moment, it's a pity he doesn't use mobile phones, typical 'old school' British mentality."

Rose said, even without looking at Anita.

The use of a mobile phone was kept a complete secret from his family members, by Michael. Appu appeared from nowhere,

"Chuti Menike, be careful, the stairway is slippery, I am going to get Banda to wipe it. Would you like to have your breakfast here?" completely ignoring Rose.

But it was Rose who spoke;

"We will have our breakfast here. First, can you bring some coffee please?" With a somewhat lukewarm gesture of a courtesy,

"Yes Madam."

He left and disappeared down the same slippery spiral stairway.

When the sunrays started to appear behind the Knuckles range initially, they were directed toward the sky and when the smiling sun started peeping gradually over the mountain tops, the mist began hiding away and eventually disappeared into thin air, as if it were never there.

Anita was dreaming of her aunt falling and being hospitalized for many months, encountering a slippery slope which stopped six feet under. Only, the aroma of fried bacon and coffee brought her back to reality, to see Aunt Rose hale and hearty by her side, looking at her tenderly. A tear fell down her cheek.

"Aunty Rose, I am so fortunate to have you around me, thank you for being my only Aunt," and kissed her hand with much love and affection. Daydream abandoned.

The creator must have had a super PhD to inculcate such deceiving expressions, whilst his creation of sorts, kept floating on absolute thoughts of ill will.

The Irony is that the creator managed to inculcate such behavior not only in one mind, but in the minds of more than nine billion humans. However, he had failed miserably to do so in other living creatures of this world.

Banda was wiping the staircase but what he really wanted was to have a glimpse of 'Chuti Menike,' and possibly exchange a word or two with her.

So, he sprang into action, brought a mop and started mopping the balcony, only to be rudely interrupted by Appu, for which, Banda promised himself to throttle the 'scum bag' one day.

He thought stabbing would be far too nice an end for Appu.

Nevertheless, he knew Chuti Menike would be coming to the stables one of these days, so he could make her acquaintance more privately.

CHAPTER 19

The tried and tested theory of 'Learn the trade first' started playing havoc in Anita's mind!

To start with, she began exploring the estate. She casually walked toward the stables. Banda appeared from nowhere like a ghost, while flashing all of his teeth in a broad smile.

However, he made sure Appu was nowhere to be seen, before approaching the 'Chuti Menike,' whom he admired and had kind of fallen in love with, in a different paradigm. One cannot establish whether it was a standard 'fallen in love,' scenario, since the human thought process is a poorly understood entity. Could have been the equivalent of a 'schoolboy crush.'

Nevertheless, Banda loved Chuti Menike.

"Chuti Menike, come with me, I'll show you Doodthal"

Anita realized that Banda couldn't pronounce the word 'Doodle', clearly.

"OK, show me Doodthal," she mimicked the word. When in Rome, 'do as the Romans do', or is it more appropriate to say, when in Sri Lanka, 'do as the Sri Lankans do.'?

As soon as Anita entered the stables, 'Doodle,' recognized her and acknowledged her with a low-pitched snort and a very gentle wiggling of her back. Banda brought Doodle into the open-air gravel area.

"Chuti Menike, she loves to be brushed." He offered a rather worn-out currycomb to her.

First, she stroked Doodle's jaw area below the eyes. In

160

appreciation, Doodle continued with her very low-pitched snort. Banda started speaking non-stop while cleaning the interior of the stable.

"Chuti Menike, Michael Hamu is a very good man. He looks after us very well. He is a very private person and does not speak at all. He is an excellent rider; you know it is a very difficult ride in these mountains. Doodthal is very good, she can go anywhere. Hamu started riding her often, more recently."

It was like a 'verbal diarrhea,' even a big cork would not be able to stop.

Anita was methodically brushing her from head end to tail end. She finished the left side and started on the right side. Then she noticed a rather long scratch mark on Doodle's mid body and she noticed the mare didn't like that area to be touched.

"Banda, what happened to Doodthal? There is a fresh scratch mark here and she won't let me touch that area"

"Oh, let me see,"

Banda took the given opportunity to move close to this gentle angel. The next split-second, Banda was only inches away from Anita. He could smell the fragrance of the woman, not just a woman but an unbelievably beautiful one, found only in heaven and not in this human world; and he said to himself,

'I can be your slave, take me as your slave, I'll sacrifice my life for you.' "Banda, you are dreaming!"

"Chuti Menike, last time when Hamu took her out to go hunting, master spent the whole night and returned empty handed the following day, in the afternoon."

"Does he go hunting very often? It is cruel. I don't like those stuffed animals inside the house." Anita remembered Ranga mentioning that he was also disturbed by those trophies.

"He doesn't go hunting regularly but within the last three

weeks, he went three times and never stayed overnight ever, except last time. On his previous trip, he had shot a huge hog."

Anita was not really interested in hunting. She decided it was best to avoid the subject and attend to the matter at hand and thought it was better to clean the scratch with 'Dettol,' since it was inflamed.

"Banda, is there any Dettol in the house?"

Even without answering, Banda ran toward the house and came back with a quarter full, 500 ml Dettol bottle. Since there was no cotton wool available, Anita asked him to bring some facial tissues.

She applied the Dettol on the wound with the tissues. "Ok girl, now you are on the mend." She kissed the mare and asked Banda to clean the area with the same daily, until it healed.

Banda watched Anita walking toward the house, while still holding the bottle of Dettol in his hand.

He prayed to God for him to get a wife like 'Chuti Menike,' in his next birth! Yet again, he knew he needed heaps of good merits to achieve such a herculean task.

Anita had a strong feeling that someone was watching her. When she looked up at the house, she saw Aunt Rose on the balcony, observing what was happening down below.

'Nosy cow,' she thought to herself. 'If you couldn't beat them, then join them,' was the order of the day for Anita.

"Have you done horse riding before dear?"

"Every school holiday, Thaththi (Father) used to take us to Nuwara Eliya Turf Club and train me to ride. As a matter of fact, I was very good at it, it stopped only when I entered Uni."

Rose was standing near the telescope, though she was not observing anything through it. "I can't rotate the telescope; it is stuck pointing toward the knuckles range"

"Let me see Aunty."

When Anita walked toward the telescope, to her surprise, Appu beat her to it, coming seemingly from nowhere.

"Let me, madam" with a kind of gesture which pushed Rose away from the telescope, literally though not physically, implying that she was hopelessly incapable of turning it.

Anita wondered why the phrase 'nosy bull,' was still not in the vocabulary of the self-claimed superior language of English.

Rose withdrew haughtily from the telescope, showing her displeasure.

The young hot blood in Anita did not want to give in easily; "let me see Aunty."

Sensing this disdain and getting the message, with a gesture of a half-baked bow and straightened right arm pointing in the direction of the telescope;

"Chuti Menike, of course you can do it,"

Slyly implying Rose couldn't do it but Anita could, Appu backed down and disappeared faster than he entered.

On close inspection, Anita realized that one of the hinges of the gimbal mechanism was tightened beyond its working range. At the same time, she observed that the surface of the housing showed an area which was unexposed to the weather elements.

It did imply though, that for quite a considerable time, the telescope had been locked in one direction and only just recently, had been set in a different direction.

Even though the women's lib crusaders claim that women can do everything a man can do, Anita thought this was one of the things you really need a man to do, like loosening a tightened nut or a leak in the plumbing!

Defeated and dejected, Appu was watching this closely from his master's room, anticipating he would be summoned to do the honors, at any time.

It was a kind of hammering of the final nail into the coffin of his hurt pride; when Anita called out loudly, "Banda, can you come and loosen this, please?"

'No appreciation,' Appu pacified himself, closed the patio door, drew the curtain completely and left his master's room from the other side, as if he was never there.

Hearing Chuti Menike's call, elated Banda looked up at the sky and said "Thank you," and sprinted so fast, probably beating Bolt by a few yards.

To his supreme bliss, Banda managed to loosen the stuck gimbal mechanism in no time. Curious, Anita rotated the telescope to its previous position expecting a better sight than the mountain range top.

However, to her utter disappointment, it was a boring row of terraced houses.

She immediately turned it back in the direction of the Knuckles Range and gently tightened the mechanism with a feminine touch, which was greatly appreciated by the mechanism.

The gimbal mechanism itself was overjoyed, as for the first time, it had a feminine touch instead of the rough 'male handling,'; making it loose enough to move around and just tight enough to maintain the required position.

The gimbal mechanism was thinking 'Why was I treated roughly like that all these years?'

CHAPTER 20

The flashing green LED light of the DIG Central Province Office electronic switch board, indicated that there was an incoming call from outside the precinct.

"Hello, this is Southern Province Police Headquarters, is DIG Silva available?" "Hold the line please, I'll connect."

DIG Silva was in a pensive mood after attending a family wedding the previous night. One could see the DIG's sleepy eyes opening wide and his back which was sagging the last hour or so, straightening up. Whilst answering the phone, he rang the modern call button which was somewhat hidden on the underside of the desk. The sound of the bell could not be heard at all. However, a young PC appeared from nowhere and saluted his superior.

"Call SSP Ranga, quickly!"

Ranga, who was going through the Government Analyst's reports on artifacts recovered from two crime scenes, came almost running to the DIG's office room.

Puzzled, Ranga looked at the DIG and realized he was not ill as he had presumed, since the DIG had appeared 'under the weather' that morning.

"Ranga, this is DIG Southern Province, I am switching to 'speaker phone,' please go ahead."

"Within the last three days, we have had very unusual deaths reported in three places, Galatuduwa, Uragasmanhandiya and Diyapitigallana. These three villages are located within around a

30 km radius. All deaths are of children between eight and twelve years old. We are still awaiting JMO reports and further information. However, we have reason to believe these deaths are similar to what you have experienced. I thought your office might be of help"

DIG Silva stood up and started walking up and down the office and shouted,

"Someone bring me a map to find out where the hell those goddamned places are situated"

Ranga wished the Southern Province DIG were deaf, due to the thunderous voice of DIG Silva at this end. Ranga finished the call reassuring the DIG they will help. "Ranga attend to it please, I have a thundering headache, can someone bring me some paracetamol?"

It took another good thirty minutes to find a map of the police divisions of Sri Lanka. Even without looking at it, DIG Silva ordered the map to be stuck to the white board at the incident room. After swallowing two paracetamols and chewing a digene tablet, he decided to stay in his office.

Ranga gathered the whole team and it was like the Monday morning stock exchange.

The consensus among those present, was to wait until further reports were in, prior to arriving at final conclusions; but to keep studying the situation, taking into account the evidence collected so far.

Ranga also felt a slight headache and a burning sensation in his stomach.

"Hello, Anita how are you? I am missing you a lot."

"Oh, how nice to hear that," in a sarcastic tone, Anita answered the phone.

However, her brain started pouring endorphins in

anticipation of a saucy conversion; scientifically known as a 'Pre-empt.'

"There is another development."

Like the destruction of Hiroshima, a total annihilation of the expected loving and flirty words, she wanted to hear from Ranga, sank Anita's mood deeper than the 'Kola Well,' in Murmansk in Russia.

The endorphin surge was brutally suppressed like the Shanghai massacre of 1927, in China.

By now, Ranga was somewhat enlightened about female behavioral patterns; so even without stopping, he changed to reverse gear, or one can say, did a complete U turn!

"Darling, I want to come and visit you." A quick learner.

"Ok, I'll send the car." The conversation stopped there abruptly.

Ranga thought his gastric ulcer was going to explode like a suicide capsule.

The thought that he was going to be with her, doused the flames of the surprised behavior of Anita.

When the Merc pulled into the carport, Anita was waiting leaning on the door frame, as if it needed a support. She was wearing a flowery poplin dress, commonly worn by the village damsels.

'Oh, my God what a beauty!' Ranga's sexual arousal expanded even beyond what the 'blue,' pill was capable of.

All the more welcome, was another leap by petite Anita above Ranga's hip, locking her legs more forcefully than the first time! Only a passionate kiss managed to release the grip and only then were her feet allowed to bear the weight of fifty-two kilograms.

When these lovers were on their way to the room, the

intimidating look of that bust of the majestic antler asked Ranga, "Hello, hello, hello, what's going on here?"

'You stuffed bully, hang in there until I fix you one day' was Ranga's animated response. The visitor's room door closed and one could hear the old-fashioned lock clicking.

The creaky overhead ceiling fan couldn't take it any more and prayed for an unseen God to put it to a permanent state of 'Status Epilepticus,' whenever this couple came in.

The mirror, after closing its eyes in shame, said the wish was granted. The following morning, at the breakfast table, Anita inquired about the latest development. Ranga was cautious with the details, eternally observing Anita to see whether she really wanted to know.

"Strangely enough, there were three copycat murders of children down South. Now we have to re-think the whole situation again. The DIG is bewildered. As soon as I get more information, I'll be going to Southern Police Headquarters.

Anita saw the defeated long arm of the law, perhaps fast - tracked by these murders. One could say she was more concerned about protecting her investment.

However, she saw a disturbed Ranga needing a woman's touch to face this predicament. She realized she was being selfish by sticking to her desires.

Then again, she knew Ranga was the only male who could bring out the woman in her.

Her mind was engaged in an almighty tug-of-war between her desires and the reality of life. The desires nevertheless, had better muscle power.

"So, that means you are going to leave me?"

Ranga thought it was better to let this psychopath twist his neck rather than let Anita inflict slow torture upon him. At least, it will be instant release!

Next day, everything was ready for 'operation manhunt.' The Police team comprised SSP Ranga, SI Pathirana and a WPC. A camouflaged exterior, long wheel base Land Rover Defender with a special solid state FM antenna and a snorkel belonging to the police commando unit, was parked outside the Central Province DIG's office.

Ranga was about to get into the vehicle when the radio officer came running; "Sir, Sir!" Ranga was annoyed. "What?"

"DIG Eastern Province wants to talk to you, very urgent!" "Tell him, I'll ring him back."

He got into the vehicle and closed the door so hard that if it were seen by the designer of the door mechanism, he would have shot himself!

"Drive!" an order was given.

The radio officer was not in a mood to let SSP Ranga leave the premises without answering the phone. As soon as the Defender was in first gear and the clutch was being released, the radio officer did the unthinkable by jumping in front of the vehicle!

"What the hell?"

Ranga wished the psychopath would twist the neck of this radio officer as well.

The radio officer then came round to the front passenger seat window and started banging on the glass which was closed.

Ranga changed his mind 'I am not going to give the pleasure of this to that psychopath, I am going to do it myself!' He wound down the glass.

"Sir, sir, there were four more deaths within the Eastern Province during the past three days!"

Ranga felt nauseated and his head started spinning but he

didn't say a word. Very reluctantly, he got down from the Defender and walked toward the DIG's room.

"Hello, this is DIG Eastern Province Shareef Mahmoud, there were four more bizarre child murders, which I believe are similar to what you have experienced.

I mean this man is sick!

One child is only four years old and they nearly caught him, but he managed to escape. We have cordoned off the whole of Eastern Province and are checking everywhere as of now"

Shareef went on.

Both Ranga and DIG Silva were not in a mood to absorb anything. It was a bleak world for these top-class Police officers, though the fight was on whose headache or gastritis was worse than the other's; and it appeared that neither of them were willing to give in.

To add 'injury to insult';

"Sir, the IGP is on the phone."

Within the next five minutes, SSP Ranga was called back to the Colombo Serious Crimes Department. DIG Silva felt his headache was subsiding.

Elsewhere in Sri Lanka, especially the media, was possessed by frantic activity. Editors had the dilemma of deciding as to which place to send their reporters to.

Wired telephones were getting red hot, not to mention mobile-using media personnel who were not having either the Bluetooth or hands-free facilities and got a massive dose of microwaves which could boil a potato, into their brains!

Since there was no communication from Ranga, Anita was feeling lonely and bored. Rose and Anita did not have much to do just by themselves and that early evening, both decided to watch TV.

Then there was an interruption to a scheduled program, with a 'breaking news,' clip showing,

"Child murders all over Sri Lanka! Police department sleeping. Await full details during our evening main news."

On the bottom of the TV screen, the moving digital bar showed the total number killed and where.

Anita looked at Rose. Then Anita noticed a SMS sent by Ranga saying 'Called back to Colombo.' Anita wondered why God was cruel to her; Yet again, she remembered she didn't really believe in a 'God.'

That night, in addition to Anita and Rose, the whole staff of the household, including Appu, his wife and Banda, were assembled behind at a distance, to watch the horrifying news.

The news started with video clips of the first and second murders, the Central Province and Southern Province Police Headquarters. The narration included a press conference by the Police Media Unit, featuring the Head of Serious Crimes Division, the police media spokesman, and SSP Ranga Fernando. They did not have much to say.

The media personnel reported people forming vigilante groups to protect their children, significant absenteeism of school children; and parliamentary opposition MPs accusing the government, claiming it was due to the ruling party's incompetence that they were unable even to protect the children of this country and demanding that the IGP must resign.

Then another 'breaking news,'

"We are getting reports of violence where villagers are stoning the police station where they failed to apprehend the culprit and the murderer managed to escape. Video clips taken from mobile phones were showing villagers burning tyres in front of the police station, shouting,

"Police are sleeping while our children are getting murdered."

That news was the beginning of the 'Mass Psychosis of Fear,' Anita thought.

When everyone in Sri Lanka was feeling the devastating sense of fear, only one person who was watching the news in his hotel room in Jaffna, was getting an orgasm of sorts, reminiscing his perfectly planned and accurately executed, mayhem.

He was proud of himself and a sense of his life-long ambition being fulfilled, invaded his mind. Still, he had one more crucial task to carry out.

He thought it was prudent to lie low from now on. He had another two more days to spend in Jaffna, as per his prior booking. He did not want to change that, since his plane ticket from Jaffna to Colombo, was already booked and ready.

He decided he should act like a normal tourist.

So, the following day, he booked a taxi to go to the Nallur Kanda Swamy Kovil. He was wearing a white 'Vetti,' and had a traditional 'pottu,' on his forehead and a pair of cheap sandals on his feet. He made sure not to speak even a single word to anyone and did as all the other devotees did. He sat under a margosa (neem) tree and watched the surrounds. It was so calm and the fragrance of burning oil, camphor, joss sticks and jasmine flowers, soothed his mind; and he drifted off to his real life which he was meant to live.

He felt he had been trapped in a useless life all these years and had broken the chains of control of the society.

He thanked the 'Voice,' for waking him up at least when he was sixty-six years of age and giving him the opportunity to prove himself.

The ravening beast that was lying dormant within Michael all these years since his return to the island, erupted suddenly with all its destructive force; just like a 'Mount Etna,' would, giving him the thrills of his life! He was proud that he was at last, proving himself.

He was re-living his performance of the last three weeks and enjoyed every second of it!

His supreme bliss was when he saw the lifeless body with the twisted neck, still on his arms. He wanted to relish that moment where he had total control to himself.

It was total control of 'low lives,' not worth living and he knew he was helping them to end their miserable lives. He had a mission bestowed upon him by the 'Voice,' and he knew he was obeying the supreme one! That voice was talking to him from time to time from his small days and he apologized to that voice that he took such a long time to oblige.

Tears started falling down his cheeks and he said "I am so sorry for the delay, please forgive me."

He repented that he failed to fulfill his duty of terminating miserable and pathetic lives in front of witnesses, except when he was small, like when he twisted the frog's neck in front of his mother. The crushing of the lives of 'lowly,' animals was only to build up his skills toward terminating the lives of suffering human beings, just as a medical student would hone his skills by dissecting animals and insects.

He knew his mother would have appreciated his work of art and regretted she was not alive to witness this.

Only a serene atmosphere will bring about good ideas.

He had to stop this conversation with the Voice and excuse himself when he saw an emaciated beggar woman and a three or four-year-old child, walking past the Kovil gate. He wiped his tears. The ash on his temple mixed with his tears was smeared on his right cheek. He gently wiped it off with his right hand and got up. He walked out of the Kovil gate still concentrating on the duo who were begging for alms.

Later, the devotee was seen leaving the area and getting into a *tuk tuk*.

CHAPTER 21

Police Headquarters on Olcott Mawatha, in Colombo Fort, was like a beehive. From nine thirty a.m., various Police vehicles started arriving and dropping off high ranking police officers. Among them were officials from the Government Analyst, the Media Unit and officers of Police Intelligence and IT Departments.

The meeting was presided over by the IGP himself and was held in the auditorium. From the start of the meeting, around ten a.m., one could see the tension mounting and DIG's of all the provinces were present. Out of only three SSP's present, Ranga was the youngest.

The head table was occupied by the IGP, Police Media Head and an Officer from the Ministry of Defense. From the very first minute, Ranga realized the purpose of this meeting was how to counteract the criticisms and not directed toward how to catch the murderer.

Forty-five minutes into the meeting, a message was delivered to Northern Province DIG. The DIG left the auditorium agitatedly and came back again minutes later. Noticing this, the IGP interrupted the proceedings and asked him what that message was about. The DIG excused himself and came up to the podium.

"We just received a message from Jaffna, they had found the bodies of a beggar woman and a three-year old child who was with her, near the main market, in an alley. Both their necks were twisted in a similar manner to the others that have been reported.

Everybody listened to this in complete horror!

Within no time, the digital projector displayed a Sri Lanka Police Divisions map on the big screen with the divisions where the murders had taken place, highlighted in red. It reflected almost the four corners of Sri Lanka.

One could see the sinking feeling on the IGP's face, probably surpassing Captain Edward Smith's facial expression on 15 April 1912 at two-twenty a.m. when the Titanic sank, though the difference was that all personnel present at this venue were not going to die 'en masse.'

The worst scenario would be the IGP losing the job, orchestrated by the backstabbing DIG's and probably by a politician waiting to appoint a DIG of his choice to the IGP's post.

Ranga realized that his hands felt cold and a sense of failure engulfed him like the dust and smoke cloud of the volcanic eruption of Mount Tambora in Indonesia, in year 1815.

He was really feeling responsible for these deaths; and he wished like in the movies, this psychopath would contact him at some stage and start playing a psychological duel, so he could twist his neck and finish him off rather than bring him in front of the judiciary, which will take years to punish him or even to be sprung by some misguided politician or 'Human Rights,' organization.

He promised himself he was going to twist this psychopath's neck, even if he had to face the gallows for it himself.

A person came up to the storage warehouse counter, wearing denim jeans, a T-shirt, trainers and a cap. He produced a receipt, paid the amount in cash and two pieces of luggage were brought on a trolley to the small reception area. Ten minutes later, a posh gentleman was seen getting into a taxi, wearing olive-green corduroy trousers, a matching short sleeved Balenciaga

Bahama cotton shirt and an unusual Borges & Scott Panama hat.

"Driver, departures terminal please," that was the only words this gentleman spoke.

It was an identical repetition of what happened three weeks ago. The tourist got down at the 'departures,' terminal. The luggage was put on an airport trolley. Once the taxi left, the trolley was slowly wheeled to the 'arrivals' terminal.

"Hello, did the Flight SA 502 land?"

"Yes sir, it landed fifteen minutes ago."

"Thank you."

Michael removed the sim card from the phone, crushed it and carefully put it in a nearby dustbin. He put in his normal sim card, then rang the travel agent and informed them that he was outside, waiting for his taxi. However, to the outside world, he had been pretending that he did not own a cellular phone.

"Sir, our limousine driver must be holding a name board inside, where passengers come out."

"Oh! Is that so? I didn't realize that, my apologies, so I came straight out. Would you be kind enough to ring the driver and inform him that I have come out and am waiting where the passenger pick up is? Thank you dear."

It was a strong 'Royal British,' accent, probably more British than the queen herself. From nowhere, the driver came apologizing a thousand times for his failure.

"Not to worry my man."

The driver felt the two pieces of luggage were very light for someone returning from abroad. "To the Cline Estate please, Hope you know your way."

"Yes Sir, only turning to your estate, I don't know sir"

"Nothing to worry my man, wake me up when we get near."

It was a six-hour drive and the passenger fell asleep within no time; the driver noticed.

Michael closed his eyes pretending he was asleep and started recapitulating his lifetime achievements. A sense of fulfillment enwrapped his mind and body like a python squeezing the victim, though in this case, this was the victim's wish. He started analyzing his near failures and perfect executions. He was elated that the 'pros,' outweighed the 'cons' by a huge margin.

'A near 'suicidal scenario,' was enacted in the Eastern Province, when two villagers gave chase and he managed to run into a nearby jungle patch bordering the lagoon; to find an abandoned outrigger canoe, then paddling with his bare hands and disappearing into the mangrove. He just felt goosebumps appearing on his upper torso, with this recollection.

'That was a near miss!' he thought.

He was glad of periodically getting rid of his combat attire as single items at various rubbish dumps and getting rid of both backpacks separately; one in the Southern Province battle-field close to Koggala River and the other in a watery grave with two 10 kg stones in it, near the Kinniya Bridge in Trincomalee. After three days in Hikkaduwa, he had left from Koggala to Trinco by aquaplane.

When he left Trincomalee after five days, he did not have any luggage and he was wearing a sarong and a cheap shirt, until he reached Anuradhapura by bus.

At Anuradhapura, he had replenished his final battle logistics, obviously paying cash. He had taken the scheduled intercity train from Anuradhapura to Jaffna. He was glad he had got rid of his hip pouch with the zip, in which he kept his cash all along, in a rubbish bin full of banana leaves in a vegetarian café in Jaffna.

From Jaffna, he had taken the scheduled flight to Ratmalana

airport and from there, a cab to the Katunayake Airport, as planned.

Mission accomplished!

This time he really fell asleep, only to be woken up near the turn to his estate.

CHAPTER 22

"Oh, welcome home, Michael!"

Rose couldn't wait to welcome her brother. Anita was also elated because without her uncle, she thought his estate was dead and boring.

It was not only Rose, Anita, Appu, Doodle and Banda who missed him, even the tea bushes, the wild life and even the garaged Phantom and the MG missed him.

"We missed you Uncle."

Anita gave him a big hug and a kiss.

"Did you manage to get any idea about the tea estate dear?"

It was a very tender and touching few words to Anita who thought her whole world will change because of this fine gentleman.

"Not yet, my teacher abandoned me for three whole weeks."

With a gentle smile, Michael took both his pieces of luggage without letting Appu carry it for him; leaving Appu wondering if,

'All this was because of Chuti Menike.'

Appu noticed the luggage did not appear to be heavy in comparison to when his master left. A few weeks back also, he remembered master carrying his sports bag into his room and closing the door. He was puzzled.

Then again he thought, 'who am I to question these things?' He really felt he was losing his grip in this household and was somewhat dismayed as to why the master was also changing.

The jet lagged tourist hit the sack immediately and slept through the night.

Rose and Anita having had their dinner early around seven p.m., settled down to watch the news with a glass of brandy each in their hands. Yet again, the headlines were about the mysterious child murders. Now the protests had spread to the Southern Province as well. The police spokesman had held a media briefing around five p.m., targeting the evening news.

The IGP himself appeared in person and briefed the public that measures had been taken by the police to safeguard the general public, especially the children. He appealed to the public to be vigilant about their children and said a police guard would be introduced to all the schools and advised parents not to allow their children to go to school alone or play without adult supervision. Further, he mentioned;

"We have employed new Police teams in each province and overall supervision and coordination will be done by my office directly. Police teams already conducting operations have been replaced by new teams with more experience in such matters."

"Bollocks!" Anita was spontaneous.

Rose looked at Anita and said, "See, now you can have your man back." and finished the remaining brandy with a 'bottoms up,' gesture.

Then reporters from four provinces presented 'live' television coverage. In the Northern Province, there was a candlelit vigilance in front of the Police headquarters, with people holding placards displaying slogans such as:

"Police Incompetency", "It's our Children", "If you cannot protect us let us do it ourselves." It was a very peaceful, yet very effective protest by teachers and parents.

In the Southern Province however, it was a different scene,

violent crowds surrounding the police stations, demanding protection and removal of all police personnel, completely blocking the roads.

However, the east was relatively quiet with police personnel wearing riot gear, guarding all police stations.

In front of the IGP's office, there was a lone protestor holding a professionally printed placard stating "Politically appointed, Incompetent IGP, go home."

One of the sentries guarding the door to the building wondered who could be the DIG behind this and thought 'whoever comes or goes, still I'll be saluting this lot to make ends meet.'

He was curious to know how much this protestor got paid to do that, whilst saluting yet another DIG who happened to be going inside the building that very moment.

Anita didn't hear anything from Ranga since he sent that text message. She was eagerly waiting to see him on television but he was not to be seen at all. She needed a stiff drink to fill the vacuum.

She established the fact that the 'vacuum buster,' in loneliness or in happiness; the companion undoubtedly was none other than alcohol.

Scientific fact established, tipsy Anita wobbled her way into the visitor's bedroom, bumping into unsuspecting pieces of furniture. The antler was pleased, so was the creaky rotator who witnessed Anita collapsing onto the bed without even changing into her nightie.

Shakespeare's Hamlet and Louis XIII de Remy Martin kept Rose company until the wee hours that night and she also wobbled her way into her room, bumping several times into the furniture, this time as expected, yet unable to do anything about it.

The breakfast table was alive. Elated Michael was wearing a bright red polo-neck long sleeved T- shirt and a black corduroy trouser. Miraculously, Anita was alive and bright, wearing her wrangler jeans and a bright yellow top. Rose was not going to be out of place either, wearing a woolen mix long skirt and jungle khaki, long sleeved top, as if she was ready to be the factory manageress.

Michael took the first sip of his freshly squeezed orange juice and looked at both Anita and Rose.

"You two are the only family I have, and I am sorry I had to hide like this all-these years. I have no heir to inherit my real estate and I believe the time is ripe for me to write my last will. If you two are willing to accept my gift, I would like to write all this to you two, now I feel I have somewhat achieved the purpose of my life.

The other day, when I was in this Songdhammakalyani Monastery in Thailand, it was so serene and I was forgiven for that dreadful accident which happened when I was small. Though on the exterior I was happy and content, actually, I was suffering my whole life because I was not able to fulfill my ambition. Thanks to this holiday, I was able to achieve my lifelong ambition and if my mother was alive today, she would have been the happiest mother in this whole world!"

He looked up at the sky,

"Thank you, Mommy, I know you are watching me and you are very proud of me, see I wasn't weak at all, I didn't fail you. Soon I'll join you."

"Soon I'll join you" moved both Rose and Anita and they couldn't hold back their tears any more.

Anita could not control herself and she got up and collapsed onto her uncle and hugged him, followed by Rose. Emotions were so intense, Michael couldn't hold his tears back either, though the 'Voice,' was controlling him.

"Let's have our breakfast, I am famished," the strong British accent of Michael led all three of them to dig into their plates.

Appu who came with the coffee, noticed his master so happy and playful, joking with Chuti Menike and the 'Bitch,' whom he had christened with that name, many years ago.

"So, are you going to be a monk?" Rose was teasing her brother "Or has that Thai massage changed you?"

"One cannot reveal one's secrets,"

Michael said in a light hearted manner. Once breakfast was over, he got up and asked Appu to tell Banda to saddle up the horse.

CHAPTER 23

"Hey, Anita, I got three weeks leave!"

Anita was glad to hear Ranga's voice. She was about to give him an earful, then again she thought he would have undergone enormous stress due to this ongoing manhunt and she must not stress him further, remembering Aunt Rose's advice that men are fragile.

"So, what are you planning to do Ranga?"

The tone and the way she said that, was very welcoming and Ranga felt loved. One could clearly say that probably was one out of the 'sixty-four wiles,' of women.

"I have to go to Moratuwa to my mom's place and spend a few days with her, I have not been home for the last six months, and then the rest of the days are free."

That was the self-invitation!

"Ok big boy, I got the drift, you are most welcome to spend the rest of the days with us."

"Thank you Anita, then I can tell you what has really happened so far. The IGP took us out from the case and my DIG whom I report to, asked me whether I would like to have a few weeks off since I haven't taken a single day's leave for the whole of last year. So, I took the opportunity."

"Ok, I love you."

"I love you too!" the phone went dead.

That night, after dinner, Michael called both ladies;

"Rose, Anita Duwa, tomorrow at two p.m., we have an

appointment with the lawyers, I am going to write my last will."

"Mr. Warnayaka, this is how you say, you would like to dispose of your wealth. On your death, if Rose is still alive, she will inherit everything with a clause that she cannot dispose of anything she inherits from you; and Anita will be the sole heir to your real estate, at the demise of Rose." This from the lawyer.

"Is that correct Mr. Warnayaka?" "Yes, that's correct!"

"Tomorrow we can sign it, please bring at least one witness with you." "Thank you."

The following day, it was done. Signed and sealed! Rose was over the moon since her brother had written everything to her.

The crow perched on the electricity cable in front of the lawyers' chambers, saw three very happy people leaving the premises in a rather unusually posh car. However, the crow was not happy to hang around since there was nothing to eat at the lawyers, and flew away.

The next day, Michael saw Anita's Jeep coming, driven by her mother's driver.

"Anita Duwa, you can always use my MG. Now I am too old for that kind of fancy vehicle."

"Oh no uncle, I want to go to my Colombo house and check it, since Aunty Rose is also here, there's nobody there to look after it."

"Oh, I see! Then you must go, why not ask a security company to look after it while you are there."

"Why didn't I think of that before? Thank you Uncle, I think I'll do that."

However, the real reason was, Anita knew Ranga would be too embarrassed to come there in his old Toyota or on his 'noisy,' motorbike.

When Anita's Jeep turned into Ivy Close, Tharanga came and

opened the gate. "Hello madam, I kept lunch for you, we missed you."

Then only did Anita realize the time was three p.m. She felt hungry. "Tharanga, you have lost some weight, beautiful, now you can find a man."

"Don't tell lies madam."

"No, you look fabulous."

"Thank you madam, now I am using your exercise machine every morning and evening."

Anita was surprised to see that Tharanga had prepared a real healthy diet. Baked fish, a salad and just one baked potato.

"Wow, now I know you really want to go home and find a man." "Madam, please don't joke"

Famished, Anita, really enjoyed the food. While she was eating, Tharanga was leaning on the nearby wall and giving her an account of what had happened after she left.

"Madam, I found what that small key in our key ring is for" "Really?"

"It opens the bottom of that Pettagama, there's a secret compartment at the bottom. At the bottom there is a canvas. When you take it out, you can see the keyhole. It fits and opens but I didn't open it fully, just checked if it worked."

Anita stopped eating, "let me see," she was so excited! "Madam please finish the lunch."

Swallowing the rest of the food in a jiffy and without even drinking water, "show me."

Anita followed Tharanga into the living room where the 'Dutch box,' was. Tharanga removed the books, documents and photographs and then raised the sheet of canvas underneath. Anita saw a cloud of dust and stepped back remembering the last time.

"Leave it."

She came out of the house, got into the jeep and drove away without saying anything. When she came back half an hour later, she was carrying a box of 'dust masks,' worn by workers, a pair of goggles and a box of disposable gloves.

"Bring me the Piriton."

She swallowed two tablets, put on a dust mask, goggles and gloves. "You should also wear one," but Tharanga refused.

"Madam you look like in that movie that shows how they put people into big tanks and gas them." It reminded her of Auschwitz.

'Allergy, allergy not only today, you can't come back ever again' Anita chanted.

Geared with the necessary protection, Anita removed the canvas at the bottom of the Dutch box. There was a copper-alloy plate and on one corner of it, there was a keyhole. She inserted the small key and it fitted perfectly. She turned the key slowly, then with a click the plate got unlocked. However, it was not possible to open it.

"Tharanga I can't open it because of its size."

"Let me see, madam"

Tharanga was struggling for a few minutes and she ran into the kitchen and came back with a fork and knife.

Anita was thinking, *Stupid woman, what is she going to do? Her IQ must be below seventy*, but to her surprise, the fork and knife seemed to work.

All of a sudden, a lidless metal box about three inches in height and almost equal in length and breadth to the inner dimensions of the 'Pettagama,' came out. Tharanga took the whole box and kept it on the dining table, then wiped it with a wet cloth so the dust may not get dispersed. It was like a birthday present being opened.

The adrenaline was flowing!

"Madam, is it money?" To Tharanga's bitter disappointment there wasn't any money. Only letters, documents and some photographs. Tharanga lost interest and went to the kitchen to wash up, leaving Anita to do the needful.

Anita took everything out and brought her hairdryer on which she set the temperature to the lowest and the blower to the maximum. Clouds of dust dispersed everywhere.

Still wearing her protective gear, she took everything to her room and closed the door. Becoming a bit inquisitive by now, Tharanga, tapped on the door and asked,

"Madam, can I bring you a cup of tea?"

"Nooooo!" the multiple extra vowels got the message across. Anita was intrigued but at the same time, apprehensive!

Could the secret drawer have already been there originally, when the Dutch box was purchased by her father or had it been fitted in subsequently? Thousands of thoughts started to flow into her mind, even before inspecting these secrets.

Why did her father want to keep 'secrets,' from the family? Yet again, now it was not a surprise that her father had a brother and he had to leave Sri Lanka due to an unfortunate accident that happened at home.

Again, she thought, 'I must not see this, I am going to burn it.'

However, curiosity got the better of her, keeping in line with the usual behavior of the female gender.

The contents were definitely 'home grown,' There were two photos, one with her grandfather, Grandmother and both her father and his brother Edward, when they were young. The other one was of the two brothers, putting their hands across each other's shoulders and smiling. There was also another passport size photograph of Edward. There were numerous receipts for various payments which were of no real consequence.

The one that took Anita's attention next, was a registered post, fat foreign letter addressed to Barrister George Wickramasooriya to his estate address.

Anita got the feeling this could be the mystery behind this secret box. It was an opened letter, sealed later with sellotape. Anita removed the sellotape. There were three letters in it.

Her eye first caught the letter from Maudsley Hospital in South London. Anita knew it was a famous psychiatric hospital in the U.K.

Admitting Consultant: Dr. Ian Stuart MRCP (Psych)

Patient Category: Private. Foreign National Ethnic Origin: Sinhalese

Next of Kin: Mr. Stanislaus Wickramasooriya

Presenting Complaint: Involvement in an accident which caused the death of a schoolmate. History of Presenting Complaint: Habit of killing animals by twisting their heads.

General Health: No abnormality seen in all physiological systems. Appears a normal healthy thirteen -year-old.

Summary of Psychological Profile as follows;

Happy normal family background. Parents extremely wealthy. No evidence to show any childhood trauma, either physical or psychological. Ultra-confident and very active in social events.

General conversation: nothing of note. Shows signs of isolation and lack of ability to make lasting friendships though helpful to others in times of need. Strong bond with only brother George. Fiercely protective of the other sibling.

Denies harming any animal. He feels it's his duty to help all animals to achieve peace without further suffering.

No signs of morbid delusions. No evidence of dual personality. No evidence to show Schizophrenia.

Personality Trait – Inconclusive to include in any type or subtypes.

Conclusion: Normal psychological profile with an 'idée fixe' with borderline obsession. Management: Psychotherapy only.

Discharge: Referred to a Private in-house psychotherapy facility. Anita's whole body started shaking!

Her mouth was all dry. It was like standing in front of a hundred feet high brownish black, tsunami wave. She felt so lonely and helpless and she knew nobody could help her at that moment.

Then she saw another letter addressed to her grandfather.

Private and Confidential. 'For your eyes only.' It said, destroy this letter after reading.

'Your son was involved in an accident, where another eight-year-old mentally retarded boy met with an unfortunate death. That boy appears to have fallen down the stairs, though there were no eye witnesses to the incident.

The immediate removal of your son from this facility is mandatory.

It was a typed letter on an ordinary piece of paper without any signature or name.

She felt a tsunami of fear, apprehension and hopelessness. She couldn't take it any more! She was screaming; "Nooooo!"

Hearing her mistress scream, Tharanga came running and started to bang on the door, like in a 'SWAT team,' type breaking of a door, for a forced entry into a building.

"Madam, madam, what's wrong, are you OK? Is everything all right?"

Then only, Anita realized that she was screaming her head off and quickly came to her senses. "I am all right, give me a minute, Tharanga can you please sleep with me in my room tonight?"

She quickly put the letters away, kept the photos and other documents back in the box and opened the door.

"Oh madam, have you seen a ghost? This house is possessed!" The look on Anita's face warranted such a comment.

When Anita embraced Tharanga spontaneously, she noticed her mistress was shaking.

"Are you all right madam?" She wanted to ask her if it was something to do with those items found in the box. Her mistress appeared to be so much shaken, that she decided not to ask.

"Can you sleep in my room tonight Tharanga, please?" Anita was begging. She knew her mistress well enough not to ask her any awkward questions. "Yes madam, I'll bring my mat and pillow"

"Thank you."

When they were about to go to sleep, Tharanga brought Anita a warm mug of fresh milk. After drinking it, already tucked in on the bed, Anita lay down to sleep. After taking the mug away, Tharanga came back and switched off the light "Good night Madam."

"Tharanga please leave the light on."

Tharanga obeyed and within the next five minutes, she was sleeping like a log.

However, Anita's plight was entirely different. Her professional and analytical mind did not allow her to go to sleep until a proper analysis of the situation was done.

To start with, the toffee wrapper found near the first murder and Aunt Rose having toffees wrapped with the same paper, needed further clarification.

Though something was missing, probability it was in favor of there being some connection. The missing link must be pursued.

The significance of the telescope direction; Doodle's nasty scratch; the children with twisted necks; were fitting in like a crossword puzzle.

Since scientists would not come to a conclusion without credible and proven evidence, Anita's mind was scrutinizing all evidence before her, methodically and scientifically.

She remembered her first introductory lecture by the Physiology professor – 'The Scientific Method.' You start with a Hypotheses and then either you prove it or disprove it.

In this scenario, one can say the scientist was probably biased to start with, due to human weakness.

Like in a Tom and Jerry cartoon 'The Devil vs Angel' scenarios, Anita started with a bias toward her uncle's innocence.

Was it a case of blood being thicker than water?

Yet again, when she realized she was going to inherit all his wealth, so much the better if it's now!

The 'Devil's package,' is always attractive and it can be enjoyed in this life, compared to the 'Angel's package,' which is always for you to enjoy after your death.

Then she realized that she was still not asleep and her mind was playing tricks on her, but she decided to endure it!

CHAPTER 24

Three days later: "hello professor, I have attended to my family commitments and the good news is, my mother arranged for me to see a possible bride also, in the meantime."

"How was she?"

"Well, she was nice."

"Do you think that you can handle her?"

"Well, recently I was given one to one training on how to handle prospective brides"

"Was your teacher good?"

"You have to ask the ceiling."

Both laughed loud, enjoying that bit of light hearted banter.

The following day, Ranga came over to her house and he noticed some difference in Anita. He thought she looked a bit uptight.

"Are you OK, darling?"

"Oh, yes I am just fine," but her facial expression presented a different picture and Ranga remembered one of the WhatsApp messages he got;

'When a woman says she is fine, if you value your dear life, do not ask anything!' A quick learner, Ranga saved his life that moment thanks to WhatsApp.

"Darling, would you like me to drive?" realizing she was disturbed, he volunteered. "Yes please, that's very kind of you"

"OK then, to your home." Only a nod.

This time Ranga had a medium size piece of luggage. Anita

was in deep thought and Ranga did not want to disturb her at all.

The million-dollar question was, 'Am I going to tell Ranga everything or not?'

If Shakespeare was here, he would have thought "Why did I say to be or not to be?" I have put not only my foot in my mouth, but my whole leg in it as well.

The psychologist's mind was like the devil's workshop, indiscriminate thoughts flying all over the place, though like 'Ying and Yang' there was a balance, that meant; no decision.

That did not help Anita at all on how to come out of this emotional torture inflicted upon herself by discovering those letters.

She wished she had never seen those secret documents!

Ranga was very nervous driving Anita's jeep. He concentrated on his driving, making sure there wouldn't be any mishaps on their way to Anita's mother's place. Ranga liked this jeep very much, since all these years he had been driven around in Mahindra jeeps and rather clapped-out Land Rover Defenders.

As usual, Helen gave them a loving welcome.

However, Ranga thought the Grandfather was more sarcastic this time, whilst on their way to the guest's room. Yet again, he promised that he was going to make love to Anita in front of it one day! Grandfather was not giving in either, it chimed six times loudly, announcing that the time was six in the evening.

The following morning at ten past six in the morning, the guest room doors opened and Anita walked toward the kitchen.

Nosy Grandfather was inquisitive 'This is the first time I have seen that door opening so early."

When Anita was about to make a cup of coffee for herself, Ensa came running, wiping the sleep crust in her eyes and readjusting her lungi;

"Chuti Menike wait, I'll make it; can I make one for master also?

No answer. With the steaming mug in her hand, Anita walked on to the lawn and started pacing up and down whilst sipping the coffee.

A few minutes later, Ranga realized Anita was not in the room and opened the curtains to see her outside on the lawn.

As soon as he came out of the room, Grandfather the bully, chimed a low-pitched half hourly insult "Hey 'macho man', you couldn't open the chastity belt; could you?"

He was not in a mood, even to offer an insult when Ensa appeared from nowhere, with a steaming hot cup of freshly brewed coffee for him.

Ranga was pleased when Anita greeted him with a pleasant sounding "Good Morning."

Thirty minutes later, the gravel road inside the estate had to bear a 52 Kg weight followed by a 76 kg weight, about thirty meters behind.

The flat boulder which was lying there stationary for millions of years at an advantageous place with a view inside the estate, experienced a human touch for the first time. With much excitement, it was all ears.

"Ranga, I am so sorry, it is nothing to do with you, I beg you not to ask me anything. When the time is right, I'll tell you all about it. You know I love you don't you? Please bear with me, I don't want to lose you."

The boulder learned the very first lesson of human behavior. The smaller one only speaks; the big one only listens; then the smaller one gives a kiss on the cheek of the bigger one and walks off, whilst the heavy one just sits there looking and doing nothing.

CHAPTER 25

"Rose, I have to go to Colombo for a few days, tomorrow I am taking the 'Phantom', If you wish, ask Anita and Ranga to come here, I'll be back in a few days," Michael sounded rather businesslike.

When the old security guard at the Bank of Ceylon headquarters branch, saw a very unusual car pulling in, he remembered Queen Elizabeth's visit to Sri Lanka in October, 1981. As far as he knew, the Queen was not in Sri Lanka these days. Nevertheless, he thought this car deserved a special place to park. He removed the traffic cone of one of the Director's reserved parking slots and directed the vehicle in.

When the elegant looking tall man with a rather large nose got down, the old security guard knew he had done the right thing and bent in half "Good Morning Sir!"

At the reception;

"I have an appointment with Director of Corporate Banking"

"Yes Sir, you are Mr. Warnayaka of Cline Tea Brokers?" A nod.

"Mr. Warnayaka, please take lift number four to the 12 floor, Mr. Premsiri is expecting you."

"Thank you."

Mr. Premsiri was not the happiest bank official when 'Cline Tea Brokers,' had transferred a substantial amount of money to various other bank accounts recently. He was especially worried when a sizeable chunk of USD was transferred out of Sri Lanka.

The old security guard felt like worshipping this foreigner when he handed over two five-thousand-rupee notes as a tip and looked in the direction of the Almighty's habitat "Thank you God, let this man's wishes come true," and guided him safely out of the premises.

At that very instant, Michael was imagining his final trophy in his bare hands, twisting it exactly 180 degrees.

The 'Voice,' was very kind to him. The final frontier was just round the corner! Once your obligations are fulfilled, one's life is not worth living. Every living thing has a mediocre and boring obligation of living and reproducing.

However, Michael knew he was bestowed with a much more exciting and crucial function of eliminating pathetic, miserable and low lives, with much finesse and refinement.

'I was chosen out of more than eight billion mortals!' he mused in self-jubilation.

Then Michael found himself turning into Colombo Hilton, close to BOC headquarters, where he had booked a superior suite for himself.

The valet, who had parked almost all types of cars, was mesmerized to see a Rolls Royce before him and thought that to sit behind the wheel of such a majestic looking vehicle, would be his dream of eternal bliss!

Mr. Warnayaka ordered his lunch from the A-la-Carte menu, to his suite. After a few hours of napping, he was seen getting into a taxi.

"Driver, Colombo Fort, Main Street."

A person was seen buying so many various outfits resembling numerous communities. With about 1ten shopping bags in his hands, he was seen getting into a 'tuk tuk.' The three-wheeler stopped in front of a sleazy, cheap looking hotel in

Sellamuttu Avenue, near the railway track. The guest checked in for two nights, paying up front with an unbelievable tip, guaranteeing not being registered and the sole receptionist was seen pocketing the total amount.

After showing him an unkempt room, "Sir, I can get you Chinese, Thai, Ukrainian or Sri Lankan girls, even Russian."

The foreigner just smiled. "Get me a Three-Wheeler," "OK sir, he knows all the places," additional information imparted. The three-wheeler, a bit disappointed, dropped the foreigner off at the Liberty Plaza shopping complex. After a short while, a taxi took a foreigner to Hilton Hotel.

For the next two days, persons of various ethnic origin, were seen withdrawing huge amounts of cash from various banks in Colombo.

CHAPTER 26

Rose watched the Rolls Royce moving out of the estate. As soon as the car disappeared from her visual field, she felt she was all alone in this world.

"Anita, would you like to come over with Ranga?

Uncle Michael will be away for a few days." That overture was not just an invitation to Anita, from this fifty-nine-year-old female but more than that, for this spinster who was deprived of her sex life for the last thirty-five years or so, to indulge in a secret desire.

She dreamed of being made love to by this hunk, and the devil's workshop was performing at its best.

That invitation was just like the Sinhalese proverb; "Like pouring bees honey in your ear" for Anita because she was waiting for an opportunity to spend time at the estate to gain very vital information.

She did not in the least think that Rose would have an ulterior motive in inviting both of them together.

Anita had to find so many answers to so many questions. According to Christian teaching, 'God moves in mysterious ways.' She knew she was given a golden opportunity, even though she was neither a Christian nor a believer in God.

The arrangement was mutually deceiving, like United Nation's decisions on everything.

Needless to say, when the duo arrived, Antler the bully was somewhat depressed, because it sensed Ranga was going to have the upper hand with two women at his disposal. Antler wished its plastic eyes were pulled out completely, so it would not have to witness any of these scenes.

In this game of 'love chess,' Anita the Queen had the advantage of moving as she pleased, but Rose the knight had the ability to jump over the other, reminding one of 'one flew over the cuckoo's nest.'

However, Ranga was the pawn! The irony was that all three, Anita, Rose and Michael the Bishop, knew they could sacrifice the 'pawn' any time they wished.

However, in this game of chess, the Bishop was more obsessed with scarifying the pawn anyway, due to an inherent personal desire.

Anita was on a mission! As soon as they arrived, she was determined to get at Appu to obtain more details about his master. She regretted that she had a brush with him.

Yet again, she knew she had sixty-four ways to get to him. She didn't waste her time at all.

"Appu, can you please bring our bags into the room? Thank you" "Yes, Chuti Menike."

As soon as he brought both bags, "Appu, how long have you been working here?"

"Thirty-eight years, Chuti Menike, I came here just after my twentieth birthday. Since then, I have been here. Hamu even found my wife for me; he is a very kind man. He paid for everything. He even built that section adjacent to the kitchen for us to live. He did not stop there; he wrote ten acres of tea in our names. Even though that area is also managed by the estate, he pays me the income coming from that, separately, in addition to my salary. He is a God to us. We are so lucky. Unfortunately, Justina cannot bear a child. Hamu sent us to the clinic also. They said she will never have a baby. Life is like that; we have to accept our karma."

Anita pretended that she was listening, though she was the least bothered about his life story. "You are lucky, Justina is a beautiful woman." The icing on the cake! Appu blushed and smiled. "Appu can you bring some tea on to the balcony?"

"Yes, Chuti Menike."

With this conversation, Appu felt very relieved.

As soon as Anita was on the balcony, she went straight to the telescope. She adjusted the telescope to the previous position. When she was about to look through it, Appu came with the tea.

"Chuti Menike your tea, where's Ranga Hamu?" "He will come, leave it on the table."

She took the opportunity to see what there was in that direction. She saw the laborers' terraced houses and she identified the area where she parked her jeep that day.

She got a lump in her throat.

However, this time, as she was expecting something similar to this, she did not react visibly and her facial expression did not change significantly.

"Chuti Menike, there's nothing to see in that direction, Hamu also was always looking at that direction, especially before he went hunting, perhaps he was looking for game."

"Yes, must be for hunting," Anita also went with the flow.

Ranga appeared wearing his denim and T-shirt. Anita thought Ranga was very good looking. "Ranga let's have some tea"

Ranga noticed that Anita was much friendlier and in a more relaxed mood. However, he was extra cautious with his words.

"So, Ranga how is your mother and father?" This was just a

damage control strategy.

"They are good! *Ammi* is upset because I was taken out of the case but Thaththi says it's a fact of life that I must learn to live with."

Damage control at its best! Though in a normal man-woman relationship scenario, ratification is by way of making passionate love; Anita was however, on a mission where she couldn't delay even for a 'Speedy Gonzales,' act.

Ranga had no choice except to bite the bitter bullet.

'Sherlock,' Anita thought today was the day she would rather get Dr. Watson away for a while, so she could obtain more vital evidence for the case and so it was done!

"Ranga, did you get your things from Central Province Police Barracks?"

"No, I did not have the time; my bag is still at the officers' quarters' room."

"You can take my jeep and bring it."

Ranga's orders received and he was over the moon since he loved to drive the vehicle, though he didn't have the slightest idea of the real motive behind this.

Two happy individuals!

As soon as Ranga left, Anita hurried to the stables. When she was climbing down the granite steps to the stable area, Banda appeared instantly.

"Chuti Menike, you want to ride the Doodthal? Her wound has healed."

Is it telepathy? That's exactly what she wanted to do. She knew Doodle was also a key witness and unfortunately, it was not like Mister Ed who could speak.

Whilst Anita was caressing Doodle's face, Banda saddled the mare.

"Chuti Menike, can I bring a stool so you could mount?"

The very next moment, Anita mounted Doodle effortlessly, surprising Banda. Mesmerized, Banda thought it was a goddess riding the mare.

He wished in his next birth he could be a God and his goddess Chuti Menike will ride with him just like this. She was somewhat unsteady during the first hundred meters or so and then she rode the mare like Valentina Truppa. Doodle was very pleased and felt as if she were just strolling without a rider.

Anita did not know exactly where to go.

However, she felt Doodle was taking the lead and taking her somewhere better known to him. Anita just began to enjoy the ride and thought she would start riding again. Doodle started with a slow walk, followed by short spells of trotting where the path was steady and wide. ten minutes later, they came to the end of the gravel road. The mare came out of the road and started walking through tea bushes and continued further on. Another ten minutes later, they came to the end of the tea plantation. Anita realized that beyond that was the jungle.

Doodle proceeded through the scrub jungle for about another five minutes and as soon as they reached a place where there were some tall trees, Anita realized that the mare appeared uneasy. She was moving carefully through this virgin forest with thick undergrowth which was strewn with rocks, large boulders and rotting tree trunks covered with moss; and muddy pools covered with thick vegetation, like an expert who had been there many times.

Doodle stopped under a pine tree and started grunting and scraping the ground with her right hoof; and in a rearing action, raised its forelegs almost dislodging Anita from the saddle.

She managed to jump off the mare and hold the reins

quickly, in case the mare ran away. Then Doodle lifted its right hoof about six inches off the ground and waited about half a minute.

Anita was puzzled. She wondered whether something was stuck in the hoof. So, she inspected it thoroughly and found nothing wrong with it. Then the mare kept that hoof on the ground and lifted the left one. Anita went round and inspected that too.

Nothing!

Doodle repeated the same ritual with all its feet, one by one.

Like a robot, Anita went round checking all four but did not find anything unusual.

There was a distinct nicker for about another couple of minutes and all of a sudden, Doodle turned back. Anita got scared and quickly mounted the mare.

Doodle just headed back home and Anita was bewildered as to what had happened and she was totally confused about the mare's behavior.

There was nothing there. So, why did the mare stop all of a sudden and raise her hooves one by one, as if trying to tell her something and then suddenly turning back. Also, why did Doodle take her to this place along this mysterious route so expertly, without even being guided by her, as if she was used to doing it frequently?

She came back to the stables with more questions than answers. She wanted to ask Banda about this, then again she thought she better not.

When Anita came inside the house, Rose came in at the same time as well, having spent some time in the factory office.

"Darling, I heard you rode Red Rum, are you rusty?"

"The first few hundred meters I was, after that I was OK. I felt like I should start riding and I enjoyed it, it's all coming back to me"

"Yes of course, you must! You were a fine rider and you are built to be one."

This conversation did not interest Anita. She was thinking of how to gain access to Uncle Michael's room.

At that very moment, the only man who could help in this endeavor, just came toward them, yet again ignoring Rose;

"Chuti Menike, would you like some 'rasam' as an appetizer before lunch is served?"

The name rasam alone, stimulated Anita's taste buds to secrete copious amounts of saliva. "That would be nice." she said, looking at Aunt Rose. Only a snobbish nod from Rose.

Anita just noticed the 2 inch-wide 'pure leather,' belt with the polished stainless steel special buckle, worn by Appu to secure the crispy white sarong he was wearing.

To a side, there was a little leather pouch attached to the belt with a gold-plated chain, which contained a large ring with numerous keys.

The keys were kept inside the pouch, while the gold-plated chain dangled in a semi loop. Anita knew the answer to her burning question was there. The key to Uncle Michael's room!

CHAPTER 27

Anita was disappointed, since she had failed to find any answers to her questions.

The key to the door of Michael's room was guarded by Appu by keeping it on his person all the time. She was getting very apprehensive because she had not made any progress whatsoever.

Ranga pacified himself by imagining that this was what it was going to be, if he were to get married. Though they made love and it seemed hot at the time, he knew Anita did not really enjoy it and he too felt as if he was making love to an inflated doll. Lately, the fire seemed to be missing in their acts of love.

In the meantime, Rose made a valiant attempt to lure Ranga into a romantic encounter, which did not appear to materialize at all anyway, maybe because her age was beginning to show. Rose knew this was her last opportunity and she resorted to the motto, 'Do or Die.'

The bully, the antler, suspected what was going on and thought it was too hard on Ranga and decided to play a waiting game. It had the patience and all the time in the world and thought 'I'll just hang in here.'

Around three p.m., when the Rolls Royce pulled straight into the garage, Rose was ecstatic but Anita wasn't the happiest. Ranga was glad Michael was back. That night, just after dinner, Michael excused himself; "I am tired, I'll see you all at breakfast." thus avoiding the customary night cap.

"Ranga, would you like to join me? I am going hunting tomorrow."

Ranga jumped at the idea since he was bored. He was still completely unaware of the discoveries Anita had made.

"Anita would you like to join us?"

"I'll pass, I don't like killing animals."

Michael was always dressed for the occasion. This time, it was jungle green safari pants and long-sleeved shirt with many zipped pockets and a soft commando hat.

Looking at Ranga's attire,

"Ranga, I have reason to believe you have never gone hunting before, for that matter, even on a wildlife trip."

Ranga was wearing a blue denim and a red T-shirt. He felt so ashamed.

"I have some hunting shirts; I am sure you can wear one of those." and called Appu. Appu brought a thick olive-green shirt, yet again with many pockets.

It was a perfect fit and that shirt had leather patches stitched in at the elbows for lying-down shots.

"Anita, do you mind if we take your jeep?"

"OK Uncle."

"Ranga, can you bring the jeep down to the estate road? You have to drive round to come to this road."

Michael walked toward the stables and called Banda;

"Banda can you bring that mountain rope?" It was a professional 50-meter-long rope used by mountaineers.

Anita's jeep driven by Ranga, stopped further down on the gravel road leading to the estate.

Michael came like a professional hunter reminiscent of Jim Corbett, though he had neither a white skin nor a beard.

He was so impressive with his hunting attire on, 'he looked

like a real killer', Ranga thought.

Ranga envied all super rich and their life styles. Yet again, he liked Michael and his suave ways so much and thought he could learn from this man, how to live a rich man's life.

"OK Ranga just drive; we can take this beauty about half a kilometer off road and the rest we have to walk. I'll take you to a fine spot about which even I found out recently"

Ranga was really impressed with the antique rifle.

"We will drive as far as possible, careful, this is not flat land"

Off the gravel road, it was not easy to drive. As soon as all four wheels were engaged, Ranga felt the power and the unbelievable ground grip. Due to the undulating terrain, thick scrub vegetation, rocks and boulders, they were not able to proceed for even three hundred meters.

"Let's leave the jeep here."

Ranga also thought it was better to leave the jeep there, since he was getting apprehensive driving Anita's jeep and finding his skills for 'off-roading' was hopelessly inadequate.

"Ranga, would you be kind enough to take the rifle please?"

The mastermind of deception, was luring the unsuspecting victim toward the bait, tactfully and methodically. The proverbial 'dangling of the carrot.'

The final crusade needed unprecedented planning and meticulous execution!

In this endeavor, the very first step was to win the trust of the 'prize catch.' 'Voice,' was kind to Michael.

'Voice,' was guiding him better than Peter Framptom, when it came to the matter of 'Show me the way.'

Then again, obedient Michael who followed not only the Voice, but also remembered 'Patience is a virtue,' in the thirteenth Century poem 'Piers Plowman,' written by the English poet,

William Langland.

'I am not in a hurry,' he said to himself whilst handing over the rifle to Ranga.

"Ranga, you walk in front, you will find a kind of foot path, just follow it, if you see something moving, shoot!"

Michael showed him how the trigger mechanism worked in this ancient rifle. Without Doodle, it was a good ninety-minute trek to the hunting lodge site.

"How good are with your climbing skills? Can you beat Tarzan?"

"I have done a course in mountaineering, which included abseiling, as part of our commando training"

"There you are soldier! It's all yours to conquer this rock. In a way though, it's too easy, because those creepers probably do not make it worth your skills"

"What do you want me to do?"

"Take this rope and climb up there and secure it on top, there is a boulder where you can secure it. Leave the rifle here."

Ranga wanted to impress. He hung the rope across his shoulder and with much skill, climbed up within no time and secured the line.

"Bravo Ace! Your feeble Uncle is impressed!"

When Michael came up within the next couple of minutes with the rifle and his shoulder bag, assisted by the rope; Ranga thought that either the dictionary must be amended pertaining to the meaning of the word 'Feeble,' or there was a question about Michael's command of English. Nevertheless, he was glad he impressed Michael.

Ranga couldn't believe such places exist in this world. Michael gave a running commentary and described everything about this vantage point as best he could.

"OK Ranga, now it's the waiting game."

Michael sat on the rock face close to the edge where visibility was ideal for shooting, handed over the rifle to Ranga and asked him to settle down with the gun. Ranga could see down below and thought that James Baker who built his hunting lodge here on this rock, would have been really clever and adventurous.

Michael took out a 24-ounce Stainless steel hip flask and two stainless steel 25 ml shot cups from his shoulder bag,

"Ranga would you care for a drop of Port? Good to kill time even if you can't kill anything else. This is Croft Reserve Tawny port; I get a regular supply from the U.K."

Ranga had never heard of port and didn't have an idea of what it was. However, from the aroma and the container it was kept in, he knew it was some kind of alcohol and pretended he knew.

"Yes, Michael you got the taste for it?" With this, he consolidated his knowledge about alcohol. His whole thought process was hell bent on protecting his pride and it was doing a pretty decent job, so far.

"So, you like it? I am the odd man out; it is always bottoms up for me. Today, you can learn a few tricks of the trade."

Michael filled both cups. Gave one to Ranga,

"Cheers, in memory of James Baker who built this here."

"Bottoms up for Michael, who re-discovered the place." and Ranga followed suit. Ranga couldn't believe the taste he experienced. He guessed it was some kind of 'ritzy' wine and he liked it!

"Ok big boy, now let's look for game," Michael handed him over a pair of binoculars.

"You know how clever that hunter was? From this point, even if you talk loud, animals wouldn't hear anything because of the height. However, if you are at the same level as the animals down there, they can sense even a whisper".

Ranga thought he had so much to learn from this genius. After three bottoms-ups within the next fifteen minutes, Ranga noticed a huge wild hog with fearsome tusks which were about 4 inches long and curved upwards. He signaled to Michael, pointing to the fine specimen and took a prone position with the rifle pointing toward the animal. Then only Ranga realized the value of the leather patches at the elbow joints.

To Ranga's ecstasy, the shot he fired, smashed the wild hog's head into smithereens. A loud clap was followed by a shout of;

"Bravo, Bravo, Bravo," and a solid hand shake. Ranga was over the moon!

He knew he had impressed Michael without any doubt. However, Michael on the other hand, reveled in the fact that the first phase of 'Operation Ranga,' was successfully completed.

A successful day for both.

"Ranga, we can leave the rope as it is, no one bothers to come this way, anyway. Let's go back. Usually, I never take my game to the bungalow, I give it to the staff at their quarters."

Ranga really wanted to take his trophy with him, then again realized that Anita was not keen on hunting and to show Michael that he also preferred hunting only as a sport, responded half-heartedly, "Yes, that's an excellent idea."

'No point taking a headless trophy home anyway,' he mused.

CHAPTER 28

Anita was debating the whole day, whether she should tell Ranga or not. In the meantime, the two hunters came home in a jubilant mood. When she saw the camaraderie they had built up, her suspicious thoughts tortured her like the Roman candles used by Nero on Christians at their garden parties, held within the Imperial Gardens. She simply couldn't handle herself!

"Ranga is a crack shot!"

"Oh, its beginner's luck," Ranga played it down. Anita completely ignored the conversation. Michael also realized it and changed the subject completely.

"Shall we play Bridge this evening?" Michael suggested. Opportunity knocked and the answer came from Rose.

"What a good idea! My partner is Ranga."

"Aunty Rose, I have never played it before." Ranga said and the honest truth was, he had never heard such a card game existed.

"Don't worry dear, I will teach you," with a penetrating flirty look, Rose assured Ranga, which was casually noticed by Anita.

"I am sure this muscle-man must be having an equally big brain," Rose came close and squeezed Ranga's strong biceps.

"Aaawww, Aunty it hurts!" came Ranga's teasing rejoinder.

Anita was not in a mood for all these. She just left the area without uttering a single word!

Though Ranga noticed Anita was ignoring him, by this time he was accustomed to her moods. He was more concerned about becoming buddies with Michael. However, he noticed Aunt Rose's advances toward him.

The male animal instinct of the 'Genes Donor,' kicked in.

When Rose turned back and walked toward the lounge area, he couldn't resist looking at her rhythmically undulating rear view. His testosterone levels began overflowing and he did welcome the thought and the sensual sight before him.

Subconsciously, he thought she was good looking and she had a different kind of sex appeal. It was better than the snake tempting Adam to eat the apple, by far.

Then Rose turned her head back momentarily and instantly looked forward again in an alluring way, swaying her hips exaggeratedly while walking toward the lounge area and Ranga was glad Anita was not to be seen.

That evening, one corner of the 18-place dining table was designated as the place for playing 'Bridge.' Then Michael realized Anita was not interested in playing a game of cards. His manipulative ways came into play.

"Hey Anita, don't be a 'spoil sport'."

"Come, you are my partner, let's show who's better, the Professor or the Officer."

The way he put it, Anita couldn't say no. "OK, Uncle."

Of course, Rose came dressed for the occasion. A low cut sleeveless long dress exposing a substantial part of her cleavage, heaps of fancy jewelry, blood red lipstick and a silk shawl.

However, Cochine White Jasmine & Gardenia perfume, out-performed her whole attire by millions of miles when it came to seducing Ranga.

Rather than sitting in front of her partner Ranga, Rose came and sat beside him; more so, to let him wallow in her release of estrogens.

"Ranga, let me explain the game." Ranga's olfactory system was overwhelmed and started firing nerve impulses which saturated his brain cells with nothing but the 'Fragrance of Seduction.'

His brain cells did not have any other alternative but to comply. It was like glue sniffing, but probably one thousand percent more powerful and delectable!

His recollection of Anita's fragrance was overridden by many times and his brain cells re- booted the system to 'Fragrance of Rose.'

These paraphernalia were only Rose's materialistic weaponry, not forgetting her inborn gift of being a woman with another 64 wiles in her arsenal.

Rose's tactic was to stay close to Ranga as long as possible, before moving to the opposite side, as his partner.

"You know Ranga, this is a true English game started in the sixteenth century, played between two teams consisting of two players at a time representing each team, referred to as a 'pair.' Partners sit opposite each other. There are many different systems adopted in playing bridge. This one is called 'Contract Bridge.' The dealer serves all fifty-two cards in the deck to the four players clockwise, face down. Once all the cards are dealt, we will all have thirteen cards each. They have to be sorted and held in your palm in a certain order without anyone else seeing your 'hand.' First come the suits ranking in order of their superiority, as Spades, Hearts, Diamonds and Clubs. Then the cards are sorted out in the order of their rank. Points are allocated to the picture cards as follows: Ace–4 points, King–3pts, Queen–2pts, Jack–1pt, 10 and 9 downwards referred to as the 'small cards,' do not carry points but rank in strength according to their numbers.

Then came a long and detailed explanation of how to count

one's points, how to select the 'trump suit,' how to bid 'no trumps', order of bidding, ensuring minimum points for bidding and finally, how to bend rules in the bidding etc. How to 'click,' with the partner in bidding and the need for systematic playing of cards, as well as coordinating with partners in obtaining maximum 'tricks' and winning 'games,' and 'rubbers,' were also clarified.

Ranga appeared 'flummoxed,' and in a trance.

Whether he retained anything about the game was highly debatable. Nevertheless, he was savoring the occasion, feasting his eyes on the alluring seductress rubbing shoulders and thighs against him; definitely absorbed in the heady fragrance of Rose, giving his libido a tremendous boost.

Anita just ignored everything. She had more pressing thoughts on her mind.

"To keep our spirits up to suit the occasion, we can drink some Rum tonight. I have a bottle of Havana Club Máximo Extra Añejo and my own recipe for a cocktail."

Michael rescued Rose by way of buying time for her to complete her tuition lesson. "Come on Anita, give me a hand." Anita obliged instantly.

Everyone agreed that Michael's Rum cocktail was out of this world! Michael had to make another serving of the cocktail as everyone was eager for 'seconds.' Thanks to the rum, everyone enjoyed the game of bridge immensely, albeit in an intoxicated fashion. Of course, with just one lesson under his belt, Ranga could not be expected to match up to the others, any way!

Dinner was yet again grand and Ranga noticed Anita was very quiet. As soon as the dessert was over, Anita excused herself and went to bed.

After dinner, over a cup of coffee;

"Ranga, tomorrow at six thirty a.m., we are leaving again for hunting. The estate field officer told me they had sighted a herd of sambar including a majestic looking antler, at the edge of the forest. You can add that trophy to my collection. I have asked Appu to make sandwiches for us to take on the trip."

Ranga was overjoyed. He felt he was part of this high-class family and he visualized his trophy by the side of Michael's. When he was walking back to the room, he stared at 'antler the bully,' and said, "You wait there mate, my own beauty will be your companion who's going to break your antlers to pieces, you big bully."

Anita was in deep thought, wondering how life unfolds itself. She was not sure where she stood. She was debating whether all the males were fickle like this or if Ranga was only after her money.

She remembered it was his voice that triggered all this.

Then again, her mind started pestering her as to whether she was really in love with this man or whether she would find love at all in her lifetime, like her Aunt Rose.

However, she did not feel any anger toward Aunt Rose at all.

Her confused mind even found a solution for this predicament; maybe by mutually using him as a stud between them, to fulfil their sexual needs.

Then again, her mind tortured her, recalling the things she had done during her early twenties, when she went to U.K for her postgraduate studies.

She remembered using all the handsome male students in her University, just to satisfy her craving for sexual pleasure. She was not happy with just one, and had wild flings with quite a few of them, whom she could not even recall now. To her, most of them were merely 'one-night stands.'

Her sexual sadistic practices could be described as a modern-day 'Marques de Sade,' model.

Her victims simply kept quiet due to the 'shame factor,' and the damage it could inflict on their male egos. They just simply kept their frolics as a secret.

They had even christened her with the name "Bombay Chilli." Only boys who called her Bombay Chilli knew what it really meant!

However, the turning point of her behavior was when her batch mate, Jonathan, who fell in love with Anita, found out her clandestine wild affairs with many students and in his rage, had slaughtered her current paramour in her own bedroom and purportedly hanged himself in remorse, in his dorm room.

She had been suspected of being an 'accessory after the fact,' involving this gruesome murder, as it had taken place in her room.

However, after a thorough investigation, the police had cleared her of any complicity in the crime.

This had led her into giving up all social contacts and to concentrate on getting through her exams and eventually leaving for Sri Lanka on a permanent basis; where she settled down to a normal and responsible way of life, till Ranga appeared on the scene.

There was another dark side to her personality, where in her university days, she had started experimenting in drugs, including hallucinogens and stimulants and was becoming 'hooked' on them; till her slain 'lover' influenced her into following a detoxification process that had helped wean her out of her 'habit.'

Even that did not deter her from continuing in her ways, proving these were personality disorders aptly described by

218

medical literature though she never really got addicted.

However, one could say she changed her ways to a much milder form of narcissistic sadism in comparison to what she was before.

With all these thoughts, that night, the creaky fan got yet another fit, proving that personality disorders may be controllable, but incurable!

CHAPTER 29

The IGP sighed due to the hopelessness of the situation and consulted the Police Special Operations head, to whom he had entrusted the handling of, 'Operation Twister,' which was nicknamed after this killer.

"Sir, we have a heap of information and good CCTV footage of the suspect, but we were not able to identify him at all, not even a clue as to who he is. A very cunning person, in every CCTV footage his face cannot be seen; always wearing a cap or a hat and looking down. Nevertheless, we know he is about 5'11" tall, chest size 42" and probably wearing size 9 shoes. Our AI programs matched him as the same person who killed the victims in all four districts. Unfortunately, there are so many loose ends."

"So that means still we don't know?"

"You are correct, Sir."

"Our main puzzle is how this killer traveled from South to East and then to the North, within a matter of hours. It seems an impossible task, even if you drive a vehicle or ride your own motor bicycle. The rest of the time-frames are well within any transportation method. Could there be a network of killers? But then, only a solitary suspect had been sighted at many reported incidents."

"Send me the detailed report, ASAP."

The IGP was happy that since he took over, the killings had stopped and most probably his job was saved thanks to this killer stopping the mayhem.

The IGP thanked the God whom he had clandestinely visited and asked for help to keep his job. Now he had to part with a substantial amount of money to the shrine, which he promised in front of this God; to donate by way of Gold if his job was saved. The soothsayer who recommended this shrine to him had told him to make a vow at that shrine and the killings will stop. He had duly made the vow and the killings had stopped.

However, he was reluctant to ask the God of that same shrine to help him to catch the killer, since he would have to make another very expensive vow. He could ill afford it.

The IGP called for another highly classified meeting among the Police IT head, Media Unit head and himself on how to release a communique to the press, showing their success without jeopardizing his position. He wanted it to be highly technical in nature, to reflect the capabilities of the Police Department under his command.

The irony was that the recognition of a human by an AI program without facial features, was yet to be developed.

The IGP thought he would approach the God directly himself, instead of dealing with the shrine, pleading that this killer would not kill again; since his previous attempt was so expensive.

He promised the God he would give up smoking if this killer stopped these killings, which was by far cheaper and healthier for him.

Then again, he asked permission just to smoke only one cigarette after a heavy meal of rice, as a personal favor, since he had already promised to donate a massive sum in gold, for the original request.

CHAPTER 30

Anita woke up around seven a.m., to see 'creaky fan,' creaking away slowly and happily with Ranga missing from the room.

Then she realized that he was supposed to go hunting together with Uncle Michael that morning. Since the outside temperature was somewhat cool at around 20°C, she covered herself with the woolen dressing gown and went up to the balcony, climbing the spiral stairway which was slippery due to the condensed mist on the steps.

She inspected the road leading to the estate, to find it was deserted. She knew that the duo must have gone already to kill more.

She thought, '*How come that every time, as soon as anyone comes to the balcony, Appu appears instantly.*'

"Chuti Menike, you like tea or coffee or do you want me to bring your breakfast straight away?"

"Appu I'll have my breakfast, thank you."

Appu carried out his routine of wiping the chairs and then disappeared through the staircase.

The cold was a soothing sensation to her and she was suddenly engulfed with the distant memories of her wild past.

She imagined male slaves in chains dressed only in loin cloths and Anita, 'the modern-day Cleopatra,' whipping them with a buckskin whip. When she was about to get the supreme bliss of beating all the slaves, who unaccountably happened to resemble Ranga,

She heard a loud cry and the sound of crashing cups and saucers from the direction of the spiral staircase; abruptly interrupting her reverie.

"Chuti Menike please help," It was Appu who was crying out in pain. "Oh my God, Appu, are you OK?"

She virtually ran toward the stairway to see Appu at the bottom; drenched by hot coffee, surrounded by the toppled ebony tray and smashed cups and saucers, with her breakfast spread on the floor.

When Anita reached the bottom of the stairs, she noticed that Appu's right ankle was twisted with the severed bone jutting out of a bleeding open wound.

Appu was in agony and she could see the frightened look on his face. Blood was spurting from the open wound and Anita quickly folded the coffee-soaked cotton napkin and pressed it where the blood was gushing out. With this commotion, both Justinahamy and Rose came rushing up.

"Justina, ask Banda to run and tell the field officer to bring the estate jeep, quickly!" Rose said. "Anita keep pressing on the wound. I'll go and get dressed; we have to take him to the hospital." Within the next five minutes, a few estate workers and the field officer, came with the estate jeep. "Anita I'll go with Justina to the hospital," Rose kept her cool and took charge of the situation.

Whilst they were preparing to take him, Anita made a splint and secured the ankle area to hold the bone somewhat in place, while Justina was shown how to press the correct spot to suppress the bleeding. Appu was shifted onto a big plank and carried away by the estate workers and placed on the floor of the jeep, with Justina squatting beside him continuing to press on the wound. Rose climbed on to the passenger seat and the patient was dispatched to the hospital within the next few minutes.

The estate workers went back to the factory amidst a cacophony of voices and Banda and Anita were left behind.

Anita was in a state of shock! 'Hopeful,' Banda came up to Anita; "Chuti Menike, there's lot of blood, shall I clean it?"

Even without thinking "Yes, go ahead and clean it."

There wasn't anyone at home, except Anita and Banda. She just sat on a bench nearby and was imagining what had happened just now. Anita saw Banda carrying the mop and the bucket. After a few minutes, Banda came running.

"Chuti Menike, Chuti Menike, Appu's Key ring is here, he must have dropped it when he fell."

"OK, leave it on the dining table."

She was not absorbing any of this, since she was in deep thought regarding the predicament they were in. She thought this house would just come to a standstill without Appu,

It was too much for this confused Professor to handle. Since the previous evening, her mind was playing games and in 'chess parlance', she knew it was a 'Checkmate.'

For the very first time in her life, she felt hopeless, worthless and all alone.

She simply did not know what to do. She just walked back to her room, thinking of lying down for a while till her mind settled. While passing the dining table, by chance, she happened to notice Appu's key ring with all the keys.

She looked up, "thank you God!" grabbed the keys and ran upstairs.

It was her dreams come true, though it was not under the pleasantest of circumstances! She was highly excited at the prospects the keys offered and her hands were cold and trembling when she opened Uncle Michael's room door. As soon as she entered, she saw the big map and the smaller road map of Sri

Lanka, with red dots marked in four places.

On a shelf there was the same 'telltale' tin of toffees. Most probably a gift from Aunt Rose. She froze.

"Oh my God, Rangaaa!" it was a spontaneous cry.

Then like a woman gone berserk, she started ransacking the room indiscriminately. Under the bed she found a shoulder bag which contained Doodle's Sambar skin hoof covers and another similar bag with other disguises. She did not want to know anything else.

She charged out of the room like a Greyhound out of a trapdoor and dashed toward the stables. By this time, Banda was still mopping up the area.

"Chuti Menike, Chuti Menike," to no avail!

Anita ran toward the stables like a bullet. Banda dropped the mop and ran behind her. Without wasting any time, he saddled up Doodle. There was no time to fit on the reins and Anita mounted the mare just holding on to the Mane.

"Please take me to 'Hamu,' quickly," pleaded Anita in an enticing voice expressing the urgency of the moment.

Then it was the ghost of Red Rum, on a frenzied gallop. Banda just watched 'Doodthal,' disappearing with his Goddess.

If 'Winning Brew' saw this Red Rum on that day, it would have given its retirement papers in then and there! Anita saw the jeep tracks and followed them.

Michael was carrying a medium sized backpack which was full and a picnic basket containing sandwiches, a coffee flask and a picnic mat. Once they reached the hunting spot near the edge of the rock, Michael took out the picnic mat and spread it on the ground. Then he took out two coffee mugs and kept them beside the flask and sandwiches.

"So, Michael, today you came well prepared, you know the

art of how to kill, don't you?" Ranga joked.

"One has to master one's skills, hasn't one?" The British accent.

Michael poured himself a mugful of coffee from the flask, grabbed a sandwich and stood up. "Help yourself Ranga"

Ranga was seated and already scanning the area eagerly with the binoculars.

Michael started munching on the sandwich and pretended he was sipping the coffee. However, he did not drink any coffee at all.

"I need to pee,"

Michael walked away from Ranga toward the remnants of the old hunting lodge and carefully emptied the coffee into the thick undergrowth, without being seen by Ranga.

Michael came back and sat near Ranga, asked for the binoculars and inspected the area down below. Ranga poured a mugful of coffee for himself and started sipping it whilst taking bites of the sandwich.

"Michael, Appu knows how to make strong coffee, this is good!" Ranga commented. "Careful, it can even kill you."

"Yes Michael, I have heard strong coffee can increase your heart rate and cause abnormal heart rhythms, sometimes."

"But I don't think this coffee will kill you like that" retorted Michael in an amused manner. "Ha, Ha, Ha," both laughed.

'Voice,' was very pleased with the 'final frontier' preparations. The sedative 'midazolam' that Michael obtained from a pharmacy in the Colombo Fort area, according to the literature, must start working in approximately thirty minutes time. He bought thirty tablets of 7.5mg; a month's supply for an insomniac. He assumed that the pharmacist did not suspect anything, since it was only a month's supply of sleeping pills for a foreigner who had lost his prescription. So, it was 225mg of the drug in 750ml of Appu's strong coffee. Being a perfectionist, Michael calculated the mug's capacity as 350ml. Then it would work out to one mugful containing approximately 100mg. He knew an average dose of 7.5mg was sufficient to sedate an average human being.

Michael was delighted when Ranga drank the whole mug.

"Ranga, I get constipated if I drink a lot of coffee, you know my age is catching up. You can have the rest "

"Thank you, I love coffee, it stimulates every damn thing in your body, I need every bit of enhancement to cope these days." Both laughed.

"Be my guest, help yourself to the rest of the coffee."

Voice thought it was moving so perfectly that it did not deserve to work out with so much ease; needed, a stronger challenge for the 'final bliss.'

"Ranga, we are not going to shoot anything else but a full-grown antler, we need enormous patience. Antlers live alone and usually they follow female herds. They are very cautious, elusive and hardly ever come out to open spaces. We may have to come a few days to get the specific one we want."

"I am going to relax,"

Michael lied down next to Ranga who was drinking the last bit of coffee while having another sandwich. Michael kept his backpack which contained bundles of cash and various disguises as his pillow and closed his eyes.

The Voice helped him to reminisce his illustrious life with a purpose, compared to other miserable common mortals.

'I was born for a noble cause and I was happy I was the chosen one.' he mused.

'The very first time I was able to show my calling to my

227

mother was by twisting the dirty, slimy miserable frog's head. It was the inauguration of my noble cause. The cat was a kind of 'heat of the moment,' incident. Then the goat was a tough one and I nearly underestimated the job before me.

My 'coming of age,' was crowned by twisting the neck of the boy who bullied my dearest brother. Jumping up and twisting the head needed enormous skill, especially due to my immature age and size; but I did that with flying colors.

When I was in the U.K, I had to help that miserable mentally retarded boy. He was begging for it and you know I'll always oblige because it is my duty to do so.

I twisted the head and pushed him down the stairs as prompted by you. It was very rewarding to see the lifeless body rolling down the stairs.

'Thank you Voice, you opened up the world of bliss to me, showed me the way and gave me the strength.

See, this whole world was turning against me for doing my fair share on behalf of the whole of mankind!

So, I had to lie low all these years with unimaginable patience; only the chosen one can sacrifice so much and I am very proud of myself for being able to wait patiently for such a long time.

I know you gave me the command to go ahead when it was right. I always knew you did the best for me. So far, I have fulfilled my obligations toward humanity, as you have ordained.

This particular one is for my own satisfaction; 'the icing on the cake,' so to speak. I hope you will approve this for me. I deserve this for all my faithfulness to you.

I just wanted to enlighten you; I took the liberty of arranging my future endeavors on my own' The Voice agreed and blessed him.

"Doodle take me to 'Hamu,'

Anita told the mare as soon as she saw the parked jeep. A low grunt indicated that the mare understood the request. Doodle followed the fresh footpath created by the hunters. As soon as they reached the area with the big trees, Doodle stopped. Without the reins, Anita knew she wouldn't stand a chance if the mare reared.

"No, Doodle no," Anita purred.

Doodle turned her neck. Anita leaned forward and rested herself on the mare's neck and caressed its face below the eyes.

"Please, Doodle, quickly take me to him," and kissed the mare.

To her surprise, she emitted a very high-pitched neigh and rather prolonged grunts, probably indicating,

'OK, OK, keep your hair on, I'll take you to him but where are my boots?'

"Good girl, I'm sorry, I don't understand what you want but please take me to 'Hamu." Doodle walked forward briskly but cautiously.

Anita's mind was galloping at god's speed, re-living the interaction she had with Ranga.

'In my whole life, Ranga was the only real male who knew how to satisfy me. What a gentleman was he? Sorry Ranga, for treating you the way I treated you. Oh my God, I am so callous, even to think of sharing you with Aunty Rose, when you were truly loving me.'

Then she saw the huge rock. She dismounted with care. She knew they were up there. When she was looking around, she spotted the rope.

"Ranga, Ranga, be careful, watch out for Michael! He is the killer we have been looking for! He is the killer!"

Like a woman possessed, she started screaming her head off!

Michael heard the female voice but couldn't make it out clearly. Then he saw Ranga holding on to the rifle and lying there with sleepy eyes. Ranga couldn't make out what was happening. He was feeling totally sedated due to the coffee he had drunk, laced with 'midazolam'.

"Michael, is the Antler there? Sorry, I must have fallen asleep, what's going on?"

Ranga felt his head was heavy and he was feeling dazed. It was like being woken up suddenly from a mesmerizing dream.

By this time, Anita's screams were getting closer and louder and Michael realized he didn't have any time to waste if he was to put his plans into action!

Michael jumped at Ranga and put a headlock on him.

Ranga was totally confused. He was in a daze and couldn't grasp exactly what was going on but hazily realized his life was under threat with this unanticipated brutal attack by Michael.

He managed to withstand Michael's headlock; thanks to the intense combat training he had undergone as a young recruit. Michael then tried to grab the rifle off Ranga. Even though he managed to grab it, Michael had a hard struggle trying to snatch the rifle while maintaining the headlock and both of them started rolling toward the edge.

To Anita's horror, she saw them struggling with each other almost at the edge of the rock. "You murderer, let him go, murderer, murderer"

she ran toward the rope and started climbing while continuing her screaming.

With the effect of the sedative, Ranga was not effective enough in warding off Michael. Michael's head lock was quite strong and he was not going to let go easily. Ranga was struggling for his dear life and he managed to put one of his legs in between Michael's, while trying to twist himself out of his grasp.

Then, to Anita's relief, they both rolled away from the edge of the rock.

In the meantime, Anita was climbing the rope like a monkey and continuously shouting, this time, even pleading. However, this had no effect whatsoever on Michael. He was behaving like a man possessed, with only one goal,

"Uncle please! Uncle, please let him go, don't harm him, he is the only one I have, Pleaaase!"

The struggling duo rotated like in a 'death roll' when a crocodile grabbed an animal in the water. Gradually, they headed back toward the edge of the rock.

Michael's headlock was solid and it appeared he had gone into a permanent 'tetany spasm,' of his hands.

Ranga's face had virtually turned blue and his struggle was becoming weaker. He was fast losing consciousness.

Anita managed to reach the top and she ran toward the struggling duo who were just about to fall over the edge.

She dived like a fielder who was going to stop the ball from reaching the boundary line, in a game of cricket. She landed on her stomach, bruising her elbows and knees in the process and grabbed Ranga's hunting shirt, thus barely managing to stop both of them from falling over.

Then she saw her Uncle Michael's closed eyes and Ranga's blue lips with eyes wide open, staring at her blankly.

With the other hand, she grabbed Michael's locked hands and tried to pull them apart. Michael was so stiff, as if 'Rigor Mortis' had set in.

She bit into Michael's hand, like a Rottweiler and would not release her bite either. Her teeth   pierced Michael's hand and punctured the radial artery.

Blood started spurting out of her mouth; which sight would have made Dracula very envious, if it were present.

Not a sound from Michael!

Anita's horror tripled when she saw Michael's face relaxing and a kind of a smile spreading across his face; which you observe in dead bodies, in spite of the excruciating pain he should have been experiencing.

The trio stayed solid and stationary, locked in position like the 'lava coated,' people of Pompeii.

Anita could taste the iron in her uncle's blood. Her tongue could feel the warm blood squirting on to it.

She could see Ranga's life draining away and Uncle Michael's peaceful and smiling face. It was rather as if he was experiencing a 'phantom orgasm.'

Anita did not want to see any more and she closed her eyes. Instantly, everything flashed before her mind. Ranga's first call and the rest of their interactions, like fast forwarding a VCR. Her failure to warn Ranga when she first had the evidence regarding Michael's murder spree, jolted her conscience. Unfortunately, she had been biding her time till she had the final proof; due to her misplaced loyalty toward her uncle and thereby giving him the benefit of the doubt.

Now it seemed way too late to undo her fatal mistake! 'What have I done to this innocent man?'

She wanted to cry out loud. She saw Ranga's final breath, wide open eyes and blue face. With a sigh, her mouth opened, releasing her vice-like grip on Michael's hand.

Michael, who appeared to be in a trance till then, took the opportunity and sat up, with his blood spurting on to Ranga's face. He pushed Anita away and did what he was good at and was even expected of him;

He held Ranga's head in both his hands and twisted it round exactly 180 degrees whilst Anita could only look on passively, with the blood still dripping from the sides of her mouth.

There was no response from Anita either verbally or physically. She was just seated there like a zombie, frozen stiff! All she could do was to accept the inevitable and watch with horror, the heinous act unfolding before her very eyes, totally mesmerized and incapacitated!

Michael's face illuminated. Supreme bliss! Just like the 'Burr – Hamilton' duel on 11 of July 1804. 'Winner takes it all'!

Michael looked at the sky. "It's done, Thank you."

Voice was beaming down at him!

Then he dragged the lifeless body and pushed it over the edge, like he had done before, during his coming of age.

"Good bye, dear."

Looking at Anita, he grabbed his backpack, slung it over his shoulder and pressed on the punctured artery to stop the bleeding. He took a cotton napkin off the picnic mat, placed it over the wound, then removed his belt and wrapped it tight.

Anita crawled near the edge and saw Ranga's body lying 30 feet below, very peacefully. A few minutes later, she saw Uncle Michael mounting Doodle and disappearing into the jungle from the other side.

The Police conducted a mop-up operation of the murder scene under the direction of DIG Silva, with ambulance and Police sirens screaming throughout the area. Though the area was thoroughly combed by the Police the suspect had disappeared without leaving any clue behind, in a copybook repeat of the incident that had taken place fifty-seven years ago. Red Rum was found roaming aimlessly in the jungle patch.

Anita was completely disgusted with estate life and decided to return to Colombo to continue with her career in Psychology, vowing never to return to the scene of the horrific events she had to face.

Rose took over Michael's estate, which in any case had originally belonged to her mother; and Helen continued living at 'Wickramasooriya Walauwa.'

Nicolaus the Appu, recovered from his leg injury but was left with a permanent limp. He opted for an easier life with Helen in her estate, as her Appu.

The villagers who had undergone the ghastly upheavals, wallowed in the luxury of being spotlighted in the media, though many were utterly disappointed to learn the truth about their respected and revered benefactor, till life returned back to normal and they carried on with their mundane lives.

CHAPTER 31

'Galé Kanda Thapasaramaya,' (Rock Mountain Hermitage) was situated well away from all human habitats.

There was no road access to it. Hermits never came out of their abodes. No outsiders had ever really seen this place. It was told that even among themselves, the hermits did not have any communication. The rugged terrain and complete lack of visible road access, were the hallmarks of this hermitage.

The common belief was that these hermits lived off the nature, eating fruits, roots, leaves and bee's honey. Pilgrims would leave alms in a cave about five kilometers interior, to be picked up later by the hermits. It was believed that when nobody was there, these hermits would come and take whatever they needed.

One day, the oldest inhabitant of the Thapasaramaya was going to drink some water from the nearby creek.

Then he noticed a dead squirrel on a rock with a rather awkwardly placed head.

The End